Praise for Mark A

"An innovative writer, with a postmodern inclination for exotic linguistic labyrinths of the mind into which he loves to encapsulate his own tormented fantasies."

—*World Literature Today*

"A different voice in North American Writing . . . a very special, poignant sense of humor."

—Luisa Valenzuela

"*The Mad Diary of Malcolm Malarkey* is a bizarre and unclassifiable novel that targets, and surpasses, the post-postmodern. An Irish character in the tradition of Beckett."

—Claudio Magris

"When I read Axelrod, it means being caught in a whirlwind of extraordinary, brilliant and passionately ironic inventions and I cannot escape a deep feeling of joy: no one like him makes me travel inside the secrets of literature, in an exciting game of mirrors where I glimpse the shadows of the beloved Sterne, Borges, and Calvino."

—Steven Conte

"With a carefree and eclectic attitude, Axelrod tears up the codes and traditions of American literary traditions and throws the reader into a mocking and learned journey that can only be born from a great love for European literature of past centuries. Malarkey is a character who belongs in the pantheon of eccentric literary characters"

—Dacia Maraini

Other Books By Mark Axelrod

CARDBOARD CASTLES, Old Lion Press, 2022.

UNTHEORIES OF FICTION: LITERARY ESSAYS FROM DIDEROT TO DAVID MARKSON (Palgrave Macmillan)

NOTIONS OF OTHERNESS: LITERARY ESSAYS FROM ABRAHAM CAHAN TO DACIA MARAINI Anthem Publishing

MADNESS IN FICTION: LITERARY ESSAYS FROM POE TO FOWLES Palgrave Macmillan.

BALZAC'S COFFEE, DAVINCI'S RISTORANTE Verbivoracious Press.

SUPERMAN IN AMERICA & OTHER ABSURD PLAYS Black Scat Press.

POETICS OF PROSE: LITERARY ESSAYS FROM LERMONTOY TO CALVINO Palgrave Macmillan.

DANTE'S FOIL & OTHER SPORTING TALES Black Scat Press.

MILAN PANIC: THE LITTLE IMMIGRANT FROM SERBIA, AUTHORIZED BIOGRAPHY. Peter Lang Press.

NOTIONS OF THE FEMININE: LITERARY ESSAYS FROM LAWRENCE TO LACAN, Palgrave Pivot.

NO SYMBOLS WHERE NONE INTENDED: LITERARY ESSAYS FROM IBSEN TO BECKETT. Palgrave Pivot.

WAITING FOR GODEAU, (Translation of the Balzac play, Mercadet, The Good Businessman) Black Scat Press.

CONSTRUCTING DIALOGUE: FROM CITIZEN KANE TO MIDNIGHT IN PARIS. Continuum Press.

ANGELINA'S LIPS by Giuseppe Conte, Edited w/ Introduction Guernica Publishing.

VIAJES BORGES, TALLERES HEMINGWAY Editorial Thule, Barcelona, Spain.

I READ IT AT THE MOVIES Heinemann Publishing.

BORGES" TRAVEL, HEMINGWAY'S GARAGE Fiction Collective 2

CHARACTER & CONFLICT: CORNERSTONES OF SCREENWRITING Heinemann Publishing.

ASPECTS OF THE SCREENPLAY Heinemann Publishing.

CAPITAL CASTLES Pacific Writers Press.

THE POETICS OF NOVELS: Fiction & Its Execution Macmillan Press.

CLOUD CASTLES Pacific Writers Press.

CARDBOARD CASTLES Pacific Writers Press.

BOMBAY CALIFORNIA; OR. HOLLYWOOD SOMEWHERE WEST OF VINE Pacific Writers Press.

THE POLITICS OF STYLE IN THE FICTION OF BALZAC, BECKETT & CORTÁZAR Macmillan Publishing.

THE MAD DIARY OF
MALCOLM
MALARKEY
D.LITT

By Mark Axelrod

DALKEY ARCHIVE PRESS
Dallas / Dublin

Paperback: 978-1-628974-42-3

Ebook: 978-1-628974-69-0

Library of Congress Cataloging-in-Publication Data: Available.

Cover design by Eric Chimenti

Cover art © Alejandro Biom

Interior design by Anuj Mathur

www.dalkeyarchive.com

Dallas / Dublin

Printed on permanent/durable acid-free paper.

For Aylan Kurdi, the saddest of sad lives torn asunder.

In memory of John O'Brien, a man of many letters, a literary giant in his own right.

**THIS PAGE INTENTIONALLY LEFT BLANK
BUT FOR WHAT REASON I DON'T KNOW**

ACT ONE
IN THE BELLY OF THE ACADEMY; OR, AFTER MANY A SEMESTER DIES THE PROF

"No symbols where none intended."

—Samuel Beckett

CHAPTER ONE

Who I am, Why the Fuck Should You Care & Why is this Chapter Title Typed in Courier?*

My name is Malcolm Malarkey. My father was Leopold Bloom. My mother was Molly Bloom. (Metaphorically speaking.) I changed my name from Bloom to Malarkey because Bloom changed his name from Malarkey to Bloom and I didn't want to be associated with my father. Couldn't deal with his slovenliness. His eating with relish the inner organs of beasts and fowls. His keenness for thick giblet soup, nutty gizzards, a stuffed roast heart, liver slicesfried with crustcrumbs, fried hencods' roes. Most of all he liked grilled mutton kidneys, which gave to his palate a fine tang of faintly scented urine. If the Reader gets the allusion, an "A" for you; if not, read on. Malarkey used to smoke too much, drink too much and fuck too much. Malarkey still doesn't take vitamins, eats dollops of butter, extra slices of bread: three, four, maybe an entire baguette: right, and pisses in public if he has to, since it doesn't make any difference anymore. You see, Malarkey suffers from that most fatal of all diseases: birth.

This mad diary begins on Carmel Beach just before sunset. If you can't imagine Carmel Beach, just before sunset then google the fucking place. It's one of the most beautiful places on earth and yet, to me, what is this quintessence of dust? Man delights not me; no, nor woman neither, well, maybe not women; though by your smiling, dear Reader, you seem to say so. Imagine that you see Malarkey from behind as he stares out to sea. The shot looks almost like a postcard with Malarkey standing as a lone figure on the deserted white Carmel sands as the sun slowly sets on the horizon. The only sound you can hear is that of the sea breaking onto the shore. Now imagine your eyes as if they were a camera lens that slowly approaches Malarkey and begins to circle him 180 degrees until you see him from the front: his gray shaggy hair cut closely to the scalp, his gray eyebrows, a scruffy gray beard; he's dressed somewhat shabbily, carelessly, a faded-green corduroy sport coat with patched elbows, a fading blue work shirt, with missing buttons, faded jeans. He's pondering whatever needs to be pondered. More than likely: Weltschmerz, but not necessarily. Weltschmerz can be confused with mere pondering and confusing the two can lead to world woe.

Let's cut from the beach and now imagine the neo-classical Greek pediment of a college building that bears the name etched in peeling plaster: *Citrus City College* with the letters *Cit-Ci* dangling precariously before falling off leaving only the name: *Rusty College*. That's where Malarkey works. It is early September at Citrus City College, and classes have begun a few weeks earlier. Now imagine a panoramic view of a bucolic, Southern California college campus beautifully and meticulously landscaped with dozens of Latino gardeners dressed in Armani suits and ties (furnished by the administration) pruning what always needs constant pruning in order to give students and/or potential parents of potential students the unmitigated perception that the campus is fraught with the diligence of beauty and perfection, a testament to the outrageous tuition that parents of future students or students of the future will have to pay. That is, about $250K for four years of privileged learning.

Imagine, too, dozens of students mingling on the campus green, tossing Frisbees as others ride penny skateboards who don't care about avoiding hitting other students; still other students walk silently from class to class, heads bent, ear buds in place, attending to their mobile phones as they bump into each other, like dodgems, but without the slightest reaction: bump and move on, bump again, move more. Imagine too several professors lying prostrate on the pavement after being nailed by said students on penny skateboards. Some, unconscious, some, barely conscious, attempting to lift themselves before being pummeled to the ground once again by said penny skateboarders. Just a sign of the times.

Now imagine a classroom building sign that reads: *Morbittity Hall* named after one of the major college donors, Uriah Morbittity, who made his Orange County millions as an entrepreneur on the cutting edge of automatic urinal flushers (the Uriah Automatic Urinal Flusher) and then imagine that you slowly elevate from the ground floor of that white neo-classical building up to and stop at a second-floor window before peering into a class already in session. There you will see Professor Malcolm Malarkey standing, now

without a scruffy beard, but still dressed somewhat shabbily, carelessly, in a green corduroy sport coat with patched
elbows, fading blue work shirt, with missing buttons, jeans,
and a pair of well-worn Boston Celtics' green Converse
basketball shoes. Imagine too that Malarkey speaks with
an Irish accent, that he doesn't suffer fools gladly and,
after teaching for decades, that he rarely minces words. As
Malarkey turns from a whiteboard to a lectern imagine that
Malarkey is clearly agitated.

"Do any of you read? I'm sure you remember the drill.
You start from the upper left-hand side of the page, move
to the upper right-hand side of the page. When the line
ends skip to the next line and repeat onandonandonandon
until the bottom of the page, then turn the page and repeat
until there are no more pages to turn unless you're reading
Hebrew in which case you'd have to reverse the process.
But given the fact few of you can fucking read English the
possibility you can read Hebrew is extremely unlikely."

One nineteen-year-old student, named Matthew,
Malarkey's best student and if one were going to stereotype
people could, by appearance and manner alone, be considered gay, raises his hand in answer to Malarkey's query.

"Thank you, Matthew, I appreciate your help, but it was
a rhetorical question."

Matthew smiles and lowers his hand.

"Are you all so fucking lazy even a novella renders you
hapless if not helpless? We're studying *Franny and Zoey*
for God's sake, not *Finnegans Wake* or *Giles Goat-Boy*!
Salinger couldn't write anything more than *Catcher in the
fucking Rye* and *Franny and Zoey* or that patently stupid 'A
Perfect Day for Bananafish' whatever the fuck that is, so

don't make this superb creation of fiction out to be something more than it is!"

The students are bored, they appear to have heard it all before, and look anywhere, but at Malarkey. Some are enraptured with their cell phones, fondling them, rubbing them against their cheeks, thighs, nuzzling them, gazing wantonly at them as if they were a potential sexual partner; some are texting someone somewhere, perhaps someone in the same classroom with some life-sustaining message about an upcoming festival at Coachella or if they've tweeted recently or have they seen what Kim Kardashian was wearing on Instagram and whether there was a side-boob shot or not; one student picks his nose and looks at it as if it were a sculpture by Boccioni; another rearranges her halter top making sure her cleavage is appropriately exposed, but no one other than Matthew pays attention to Malarkey. Imagine, too, a muscular young man named Wilson wearing a too tight, Property of Citrus City College Football T-shirt, leaning back in his desk, arms behind his head flexing his bulging biceps as if in training for Mr. Olympia or attempting to impress the student with the halter-top making sure her cleavage is appropriately exposed.

"Why are you even here?" Malarkey asks.

Matthew again raises his hand.

"Thank you, Matthew; once again, it's rhetorical."

Matthew smiles and lowers his hand.

"Don't waste your parents' money. If you don't want to be here, become plumbers, electricians, masons, even pimps, just be bloody good at whatever it is."

Malarkey shakes his head and looks up at the clock, which reads 10:50, and at that precise moment, a bell rings.

"Class dismissed, go skateboard or whatever the fuck you do with your lives," he mumbles to himself.

Malarkey turns back to the whiteboard on which something has been written, something that can't quite be made out. He picks up an eraser as if to erase the board as the students file out in relative silence, some stifling a laugh, some making faces at him behind his back, as Too-Tight Wilson cockily approaches Malarkey with a rolled-up essay in hand slapping it on his fist almost as if an homage to John Wooden.

"Yo, prof," Wilson begins.

Now Malarkey doesn't acknowledge Wilson immediately, but cringes at the lack of respect. It's another reminder that students are considered "customers" and faculty are "employees" and, as a former dean once admonished Malarkey, "The customer is always right." But it's better than the time a student screamed at him across campus, "Hey, Malarkey, how's it hangin'!" as he grabbed his genitals. He glances over his shoulder with the slightest smirk on his face since he anticipates what's to follow.

"Yes, Wilson. What can I do for you?"

"I was wondering why I got such a low grade."

Wilson taps the paper on his fist again.

"Were you now?"

"Yes, I was wondering. Looked good to me."

"Right. Well, let me clarify your wonder, Wilson. Your paper is, well, how can I put it succinctly and, in a way a post-Millennial will understand . . . it's shit. Yes, that's the word. It's shit. Have I sufficiently satisfied your wonderment?" Malarkey smiles and raises his eyebrows.

"But . . ."

"There are no buts, Wilson! You don't know the difference between a Pindaric ode and a nematode! Your grammar and syntax are deplorable, and your proofreading skills are abysmal! Even your dog wouldn't eat that paper!"

Malarkey smiles and raises his eyebrows once again. Taken aback, his cockiness gone, Wilson storms out of the classroom noticeably angry. Malarkey starts to erase the whiteboard, stops again and looks directly into the eyes of you, the Reader.

"Right. You're probably saying to yourself 'what a horrible professor! Where's his understanding? His compassion? His interest in his students' welfare? What an unconscionable thing to say. These young adults are the hope of our future, the leaders of tomorrow, the intellects of a brighter Utopia.' But that's not the question you should be asking. No, the question you should be asking as a parent is this: What was I doing when my child learned how to be functionally illiterate and academically and socially irresponsible. And if you're a student, you should be asking: Since when was there a plague on the art of reading? Milton may have been blind when he wrote, 'A good book is the precious life blood of a master spirit,' but he wasn't demented."

Malarkey raises his eyebrows, shrugs, turns back to the whiteboard to erase it, changes his mind and tosses the eraser on the floor as he leaves. On the white board one reads in bold caps:

"WHAT'S IT GOING TO BE THEN, EH?"

Coda

*The reason the chapter title is typed in Courier New is to let you, the Reader, know Malarkey is using the painfully old metonymical cliché that by using such a font, which is an old-fashioned type-writer font, it implies he's a writer. Though Malarkey does use a typewriter, he also uses a computer, but since everyone likes to think writers don't use computers, but still use typewrit-ers, Malarkey typed the chapter title in Courier New to lead you to believe that it's the only writerly tool he ever uses. That's bullshit and it will not happen again except in the briefest of circumstances, so Malarkey begs for the Reader's indulgence.

CHAPTER TWO

AND HERE'S TO YOU, CHANCELLOR JONES

Imagine now, that you're standing outside the Chancellor's office—since Malarkey wasn't going to get away with what transpired in the previous chapter. The nameplate on the door reads, Chancellor J.E. Jones. Johnny Jones for those who know him best. Played basketball at Michigan State. You enter the office of the Chancellor to discover Malarkey slouching in a chair opposite the fifty-something, African-American Jones who's fashionably dressed in what appears to be an Armani suit, white shirt, and tie, and Italian, black-framed glasses; he's a somewhat robust man, salt-and-pepper hair, with a salt-and-pepper beard and speaks in a soothing baritone voice not unlike Keith David.

"Malcolm, you can't say that."

"It's the bloody truth. They don't know a thing."

At that point, Malarkey pretends he's a student and changes the pitch of his voice an octave. "'But Professor Malarkey, why is there so much ironing in Sophocles?' Ironing? In Sophocles? Right, I almost forgot Sophocles had a dry-cleaning business: Alterations by Antigone,

Embroidery by Electra, Overlays by Oedipus. What the fuck is that all about!"

"You may know that, and I may know that, Malcolm, but there's a right way and a wrong way to go about telling that to students."

"Don't tell me. Was that the wrong way?" Malarkey feigns shock.

"It could be considered a micro-aggression," says Jones.

"Wha? Micro-aggression? What the fuck is that? Is that aggression performed under a microscope?"

"No, Malcolm. Malcolm you've got to be more in control of your reactions."

"My reactions."

"Yes, you can go off in a New York second."

"Minute."

"What?" Jones furrows his forehead.

"It's a New York minute. When was the last fucking time you were in New York?"

Jones ignores the question.

"Listen, Malcolm, you're a full professor. You've been teaching for over thirty years. Maybe you've lost interest. Maybe the drive is gone. The challenge."

"Or maybe the students just feel entitled. You know how many emails I get from students asking me change their grade for arbitrary reasons. 'But professor, I gave 120%. I read all the books, wrote all the papers, I think I deserve a better grade.' In other words, they did the minimum."

There's a pause in the conversation.

"Have you ever thought about retiring?"

Malarkey ponders the question.

"Oh, right. Retirement. The professorial pasture for all

academics who are too old to stud. Have you ever thought about paying me enough to retire on?"

"Yes, well, I understand."

"What do you understand?"

"Yes, I couldn't live on a teacher's salary either, but . . ."

"But! You gave me a smart two percent rise after three decades of teaching here. Two-percent! Are you guys mired in a financial crisis? I couldn't buy a year's supply of condoms for that much money. Provided I could use them."

"Well, no, but . . ."

"But what? Listen, I don't make a half-million dollars a year like you do, and second, my ex took half my pension. The day I'll retire is the day they cart me out of here in a pine box. Or has the college downsized to cardboard?"

Jones ignores him.

"What about a sabbatical, Malcolm? Aren't you due for one?"

"Yes. No. Maybe. I don't know. Maybe. Can't keep track of time. Perhaps my best years are gone. When there was a chance of happiness. But I wouldn't want them back. Not with the fire in me now."

"Then take it."

"I'll think about it. Not sure that's the problem."

"Then what is the problem?"

"The problem is I suffer from chronic irascibility. Do you have a remedy for that?"

"Yes."

"What's that?"

Chancellor Jones's remedy to follow.

CHAPTER THREE

FLANN O'BRIEN'S PUB WITHOUT FLANN O'BRIEN

Apparently, the Chancellor answers that question, since it's not long before Malarkey leaves the Chancellor's office and moseys down to central Citrus City, which is one of the quaintest of quaint towns in Southern California. So quaint, in fact, that it's at the top of Hollywood's locations list of "Quaintable Towns" and that's why Hollywood often comes to Citrus City in order to film the "Midwest." Like shooting day for night, winter for spring. Hollywood often uses Citrus City to shoot for Bloomington, Indiana or Urbana, Illinois or Iowa City, Iowa or any of a number of Midwestern towns and/or villages in which shooting on site would raise the budget. So, in order to reduce the budget, Citrus City often becomes Bloomington, Indiana or Urbana, Illinois or Iowa City, Iowa or any of a number of Midwestern towns and/or villages.

Citrus City has a lovely roundabout with a small plaza and fountain at its center surrounded by quaint antique stores, quaint restaurants and, of course, a quaint Starbucks on all four corners in case one doesn't want to cross the street in order to buy a $15 Frappuccino Macchiato Latte Espresso with a dollop. Now imagine, there's a neon sign that flashes, **Flann O'Brien's Pub**, where, inside, you'll now find Malarkey just walking in after having had his little tête-à-tête with Chancellor Jones.

The pub looks exactly like Dublin's "Mulligan's," complete with curved mahogany bar, paneled walls, blah, blah, blah. Malarkey could go into some lengthy description of the place, but that would be a waste of words so just Google Mulligan's in Dublin and imagine it with the difference being on the walls of this pub are black and white caricatures of Beckett and Joyce, Yeats and Donleavy, as well as Flann himself. It's somewhat deserted at that hour since most people aren't drinking at 4:30 as Malarkey walks up to the bar where the thirty-something bartender, Paolo Liliano has his back to him. Malarkey looks puzzled by his presence.

"Where's Seamus?" Malarkey asks with a typical Malarkian attitude.

Paolo turns as he dries off a glass. Paolo has dark features, a square jaw, chiseled chin, an infectious smile. If one were to cast him in a film, one might suggest Rufus Sewell. His temperament is completely the opposite of Malarkey's.

"Seamus isn't here," answers Paolo.

"I may be old, but I'm not bloody blind," Malarkey responds. "If he were here he'd be here, wouldn't he? He'd be standing right where you're standing, drying off the same fucking glass you're drying off. But I didn't ask you that, did I? I asked you where he was."

"He took another job."

"Where?"

"Kansas. Topeka."

"Why the fuck would he go there? Who goes to Kansas? Jayhawks don't exist. You know what a fucking Jayhawk is?"

"No, not a clue."

"Jayhawks were guerrilla fighters who battled with pro-slavery groups from Missouri. Why the fuck Kansans would invent a bird to represent guerilla fighters is beyond me."

"Me too."

"So, why'd he go to Kansas?"

"Death in the family."

That statement gives Malarkey pause. Death usually gives one pause, even Malarkey, whether it's one's own or someone else's so he changes the course of the conversation.

"Right. So, who the hell are you?"

"I'm Paolo Liliano. And who the hell are you?" Paolo holds out his hand, but Malarkey doesn't shake it.

"I'm Malcolm Malarkey and I came in here to get a stinkin' drink. What's it to you, polo?"

"Paolo."

"Whatever. Why's a fucking Italian bartending in an Irish pub anyway?"

Paolo stops wiping the glass and leans over the bar.

"All the Irish bartenders were too drunk to work. So, what'll you have, Malcolm?"

"That's Professor Malarkey to you."

"Okay, Professor Malarkey what'll you have?"

"My guess is you don't know shit about drink making, do you?"

"Try me."

"Okay, gimme a Black Nail."

Paolo finishes drying a glass.

"Bushmills and herbal Irish Mist. You want it with or without the orange peel or would you prefer orange bitters?"

Malarkey's eyes get wide.

"Surprise me," he snidely answers.

What the Reader will eventually discover is that Paolo is not merely the bartender, but the new owner. Other things about Paolo will also be revealed, but now you've got to imagine it's a few hours later in the day. In fact, there's a Guinness Bottle Draught Wall Clock that reads, 7:30 so if the Reader is adept at reading and math then s/he knows Malarkey's been there for three hours. He sits in a booth by himself, nursing yet another Black Nail when a tall, leggy, twenty-something blonde wearing excessively short cut-offs saunters up to his booth. She cocks her head to one side as if trying to think whom Malarkey is and points a finger at him. Malarkey, in his usual Black Nail stupor, doesn't pay her much attention.

"I know you," she says. "You're Doctor Malarkey, aren't you?"

Malarkey looks up and squints.

"Yes, but only during urgent care hours."

"My name is Tiffany, Tiffany Tustin. I went to high school with your daughter, Andrea."

Malarkey smiles and nods politely, but he's clearly not interested in carrying on any conversation that could, potentially, lead him into a dalliance with one of his daughter's friends, which could then lead to a possible affair, which could then lead to a possible video, which could then lead to the video going viral, which could then lead to it being viewed on Facebook or YouTube or any other social media outlet in the fucking universe, which could then lead to another meeting with Chancellor Jones, which would invariably lead to his dismissal. After all, he's not Donald Trump and doesn't think about shtupping his daughter or her friends.

"Come here often?" Tiffany Tustin asks seductively, leaning across the table, exposing her abundant cleavage and smiling a seductive smile.

"Maybe too often."

"Could I buy you a drink?" Tiffany Tustin asks seductively.

"Maybe . . . when you're older," he answers with a smile and raised eyebrows.

"Too much for you to handle, eh?" Tiffany Tustin asks seductively.

"Not without outside resources," Malarkey answers with a smile and raised eyebrows.

"Are you afraid of me?" Tiffany Tustin asks seductively.

"No, I think you're the most attractive of all my daughter's friends," Malarkey again answers with smile and eyebrows raised.

Tiffany Tustin gets a very quizzical look on her face. She obviously doesn't get Malarkey's allusion.

"Huh?"

"*Mais ou sont les nieges d'autun*," Malarkey answers, smile, eyebrows.

"Sorry?"

"That's French for 'have a good night.'"

Tiffany Tustin shrugs her shoulders.

"Nice seeing you again, Doctor Malarkey. Say hi to Andrea for me." And Tiffany Tustin sashays away, her butt cheeks casually creeping beneath the fringes of her cutoff denims.

"*Mon plaisir,*" Malarkey answers and raises his glass.

Paolo has been listening to the exchange as have three other men sitting at the bar—who look a lot like Beckett and Joyce and Yeats—all staring at Malarkey wondering what he was thinking.

By now, the Guinness Bottle Draught Wall Clock reads 9:30 and Paolo is sitting with Malarkey in the same booth in which Tiffany Tustin had vainly tried to seduce him. Paolo, of course, is sober; Malarkey not so much and he tends to slur his words as he nurses a Guinness Bitter.

"My cousin moved to Philly from Arona about fifteen years ago. I came soon after," Paolo says.

"Didn't W.C. Fields say he'd rather be buried than live in Philly?"

"No, I think he said he preferred Philly to being buried."

"Same thing. Where's Aroma? It doesn't sound Italian."

"Arona, not aroma."

"Whatever."

"Outside Milan. On Lago Maggiore."

"I don't know one fucking lake from another over there. Are you mafioso?"

"Not anymore," Paolo smiles as if there might be some truth to it. "I left that to my father."

"So, you gave up the mafia life to become a bartender? It's a bit of a step down, isn't it?"

"No, I gave it up to be a father."

"Where's the mother? Having it off with Berlusconi?"

"No, she died of breast cancer."

Malarkey is pained by that. Malarkey is often pained by those sorts of things since Malarkey's mouth often works faster than his brain.

"Oh, fuck. Sorry . . . I'm . . ."

"How would you have known?"

"Sometimes my mouth works faster than my brain. It's a disease. Too many black mails."

"Nails."

"That's what I said."

Malarkey takes another sip of Guinness.

"Listen, I think you've had enough, professor. You need a ride home?"

"No, I have my bike."

"Does it have a seat belt?"

Malarkey pauses as if pondering the question.

"Uh, no, maybe."

"Then you need a ride home. I'll bring your bike inside."

And so he does. Brings Malarkey's bike into the bar before escorting him to the parking lot and gently tucking him into the passenger seat before gently securing a seat belt around him.

"So, where do you live?"

"Live?

"Yes. Where do you reside? Lounge? Eat? Sleep? That sort of thing."

"Around the corner and down the block, over the river and through the woods, to grandmother's house we go; the horse knows the way to carry the sleigh, through the white and drifted snow!"

And so Paolo attempts to take Malarkey home.

CHAPTER FOUR

INSIDE MALARKEY'S MAN CAVE WHICH ISN'T ONE

After several futile attempts at finding Malarkey's house, Paolo finally pulls up to Malarkey's modest, two-bedroom bungalow in a gentrified area of Citrus City and the professor tipsily spills out. Even at night one can tell the bungalow's lawn is as brown as brown can be, as are the equally ignored Torrey pines and Bridal Broom bushes—not because of the California drought, but because of Malarkian neglect.

"Night, Malcolm. You okay?"

"Couldn't be okayier," Malarkey answers, slurring his words. "Night, Polo. Paolo. Good to meet you and say goodnight to Beckett and Yeats and Joyce. Couldn't be a groovier trio."

"Yes, I will."

Paolo drives off as Malarkey wobbles toward the front door, trips on the uneven wooden porch steps and searches his pockets for his keys.

"Keys, bloody fucking keys! I can never remember where they are."

He finally finds them on the inside pocket of his faded-green corduroy coat then fumbles with them trying to unlock the door. With each successive failure, he gets angrier and angrier until he finally loses it.

"Bloody door! You bastard! Oh my God, I'm warning you!" he screams as he struggles to open the door. Then he steps back and points a finger.

"I'll count to three and you better open! One, two, three!" He tries again with no success. "That's it! Don't say I didn't warn you! I'm going to give you a damn good thrashing."

Malarkey stumbles off and returns with a tree branch and in his best Basil Fawlty impersonation begins thrashing the door. For some reason, only known to Malarkey, Malarkey thinks abusing the front door will gain him access. It's not the first time it has happened. One might think after the first time, Malarkey would have learned, but Malarkey is often reluctant to learn. After all, he's a professor.

Sometime later, after Malarkey finally secures passage, the Reader sees Malarkey, still dressed in his usual garb, passed out on a couch. His arm hangs limply over the side, a shot class dangling from his fingers. There are dozens of books scattered on the floor. All sorts of books. Books on literature, books on science, books on religion, books on physics, books on books. All sorts of books by all sorts of writers from Aristotle to Lermontov, Molière to Zamyatin. Lots of books since Malarkey is an eclectic reader. A 60s era 33 1/3 record player plays Mahler's "Symphony No. 5. IV Adagietto." If you don't know what Mahler's "Symphony No. 5. IV Adagietto" sounds like, Google it or rent Visconti's *Death in Venice* or Spotify it or just buy a fucking CD and play it while you read this passage. Actually, Malarkey will give the Reader a few minutes to bring up the YouTube video of it. Malarkey prefers the one conducted by Bernstein since at the end it looks as if Lenny's about to die himself, but it's up to you. Are you listening to Mahler yet? You really won't get the flavor of the chapter without it. Malarkey will wait for you, but here are a few of the notes you can listen to in the meantime.

Right. Malarkey doesn't have time to fuck with you since time is not on Malarkey's side. With the music of Mahler playing in the background, and from the Reader's point of view, you can survey his bungalow: a mid-nineteenth-century rolltop desk (which Malarkey states was allegedly owned by Nathaniel Hawthorne), piled with what appear to be typed manuscript pages; scattered pens and pencils; and a pea-green, electric, Olivetti typewriter* with a single page in it that reads,

THE MAD DIARY OF MALCOLM MALARKEY, D. LITT
A NOVEL

On his desk are framed photos of Malarkey and his soon-to-be twenty-one-year-old daughter, Andrea, who, from the looks of it, is an olive-skinned Brazilian beauty; behind his desk, two crookedly hanging degrees: a B.Litt. as well as a Doctorate in Letters (DLitt) awarded from Christ Church College, Oxford; an autographed photo of Malarkey standing with Jackie Stewart in Indianapolis and another of a younger Malarkey shaking hands with Samuel Beckett, who is dressed in a gray, greatcoat, baggy pants, and shoes designed by Estragon. Malarkey smiles at the camera. Beckett does not. Then again, maybe Beckett is smiling, smiling as only Beckett can smile which may not be the kind of smile someone smilingly smiles, but which is clearly a Beckettian smile known only as a Beckett smile. Then again, again it could be a Beckett frown that someone may interpret as a Beckett smile when it is a frown pretending to be a smile smiling frownly. Never mind. MALARKEY'S BEING BECKETTIAN HERE

After the Reader has surveyed the room completely, and has deconstructed something about Malarkey's character not gleaned from surveying the room, the Reader notices the shot glass that falls from Malarkey's hand and rolls across the floor before banally bouncing against the wainscoting and stops. The Reader notices the shot glass reads, "Angostura Orange Bitters" and as Mahler ends after 12'07" so too does the chapter.

*See Chapter One.

CHAPTER FIVE

THE DAY AFTER THE NIGHT BEFORE

The next day, that is, the day after the night before, the Reader discovers Malarkey in his office on the second floor of *Phigmente Hall* named after California entrepreneur and major donor, August Phigmente who earned his billions in the Orange County orange industry manufacturing orange crates for orange growers until the orange growers sold their orange groves to the Irvine Company at which time all orange groves were outlawed and turned into "apartment homes" (which are neither apartments nor homes) or made into shopping malls. Looking manifestly disheveled and not a little bit hung over, Malarkey is resting his head on his desk when there's a knock on the door. Malarkey shakes his head, sticks a finger in his ear as if that will stop any further knocking from knocking. Realizing that won't happen, he gets up from his paper-strewn desk, runs his hands through his closely cropped gray hair, staggers to the door, partially opens said door and peeks out as if the last person he wants to see is a student or any reasonable facsimile of a reasonable facsimile of a student.

From his point of view, Malarkey gazes on the woman Malarkey will eventually fall in love with, but, at the time, has no clue that will happen (nor does she), and whose name for the purposes of this novel is Liliana Liliano, and who looks remarkably like Michelle Dockery, although in the present moment, as he opens the door, she's just a very attractive, mid-thirties woman with a stack of books in her arms. If one were to cast someone to play her in a film, the best actress would be the aforementioned Michelle Dockery. Maybe not. Malarkey's not actually a casting director, so how the fuck does he know; however, as Malarkey soon discovers she's not the "normal" graduate student, "normal" meaning some giddy, girly, gadfly of a grad student who's there because she thinks it will make her something that she's not; namely, an intellectual. At that point, Malarkey looks at the Reader and raises his Malarkian eyebrows as an indication of his newly aroused interest.

"Professor Malarkey?" the soon to be introduced protagonist asks.

Malarkey opens the door completely, looks at his nameplate and traces his finger across his name. Then he looks at her and raises his eyebrows once again.

"My name is Liliana Liliano."

The alliteration doesn't get lost on Malarkey and channeling his inner Humbert replies, "Li-li-ana. Light of my life, fire of my loins. My sin, my soul. Li-li-ana: the tip of the tongue taking a trip of three steps down the palate to tap, at three, on the teeth. Lil. Lee. Ana."

"Pardon me?"

"Sorry. Name reminded me of an old friend."

"Yes. I'm an adult student."

He looks at her from head to toe.

"Oh, I can tell," Malarkey answers, raising his eyebrows.

"Actually, I'm a new graduate student and I was told you're my advisor."

"Right. Then this is an advisory visit?"

"Yes."

"In that case, I advise you to find another adviser. Ciao."

He closes the door. One might think this a rude gesture on Malarkey's part, but after decades of teaching, Malarkey has discovered that students generally don't want advice and merely go through the motions of listening to any and Malarkey is eager to honor their wishes.

Lilliana knocks again and he opens it.

"I see your reputation precedes you."

"Really? And what reputation might that be?"

"That you're an asshole," she says, smiling.

"He's an asshole. He's an asshole."

"Who said that?"

"It's my macaw, Godot. He tends to repeat phrases."

"So, I'm an asshole," Malarkey repeats, non-plussed.

"Yes, an asshole."

"He's an asshole," replies Godot. "He's an asshole."

"Okay, Godot that's enough."

"Why do you call him Godot?"

"He tends to repeat himself. So, where did you discover that I'm an asshole?"

"On Rate My Professors."

"Ah, yes that bastion of undergraduate credibility, the Wikipedia of fatuity, the Google of sagacity and the last pit stop for soon-to-be-fired faculty. Well, in that case, do come in."

As she walks in, Malarkey looks at the Reader and raises his eyebrows once again as if this day might be one of his most memorable.

"How can one ignore someone so enchanting?" he asks the Reader.

From Liliana's point of view, she sees books piled up everywhere and spilling out of the bookshelves (Malarkey knows this seems like a cliché, but, in fact, it's not; if a professor's office doesn't have books piled everywhere, then the student, whose parents will have invested hundreds of thousands of dollars over four years, will have felt cheated, so one cannot overlook the deconstruction component of that); there are papers literally stacked in gigantic five-foot piles with cobwebs draping them (this too might sound like an exaggeration, but it's not, since professors often have too many classes to teach, with too many students in each rendering their research or creative time effectively worthless and only superseded by their paltry salary); Art Deco ashtrays have layers of Cohiba and Toscanello butts in them; and roach clips litter the floor accounting for the curious scent of vintage weed. The walls are lined with photos and paintings of nude women. All sorts of nude women in all sorts of provocative poses and multicolored renditions. In one corner of Malarkey's office there's a five-foot statue of a nude woman wearing a Shamrock Green, Guinness Cap and in another, Malarkey's macaw, but Liliana is attracted to one 4'x4' dry-mounted black and white photo that shows sixty naked women on bicycles except for the bicycle helmets they're wearing. To top it all off, the "classic" framed poster of *A Clockwork Orange* with Alex peering down hangs above Malarkey's desk. Liliana seems a bit taken aback by the overwhelming nudity of it all. Malarkey plops down in his antique wooden swivel chair.

"Please, have a seat."

She starts to sit, but before she does, he dusts off some breadcrumbs that had been there since the late 60s.

"Sorry. Baguette remnants from the last time Rimbaud visited."

"Rimbaud?"

"Yes, he came for advice about poetry."

"And what did you tell him?"

"More money in selling firearms in Ethiopia."

"I see. Are you a nudist?" she asks still surveying the pervasive nudity on the walls.

"No, but I'm a naturalist. So, what can this asshole do for you? Aren't you a bit old for grad school?"

"Aren't you a bit old to be asking that question?"

"Right. I'm sure there's a bloody law against saying that so please don't report me to the administration. I spend too much time there as is, so let me rephrase that question in a more politically correct way: why do you want to study literature?"

Malarkey cups his chin in his hand and looks at her, blinking his eyelids and feigning interest in the answer.

"Because I like to read and write."

"Right. Well, toss in finger painting and you've got a hat trick."

Liliana ignores him. She's heard the tales from other graduate students, read about him on the internet, overheard other professors and secretaries making disparaging comments about him, knows about his Malarkeyisms blah, blah, blah.

"I was told you're the expert in post-modern fiction."

"Nope, don't know a fucking thing about it. Forgot most of it in the late sixties. Too much time with Kesey and Southern and Brautigan . . . on the bus," Malarkey smiles and gestures as if he's toking.

"I see. That's not what I was told."

"Who told you that?"

"Professor Rabinowitz."

"Rabinowitz?"

"Yes."

"He's an asshole."

"He's an asshole," replies Godot. "He's an asshole."

"Sorry for that. Please excuse Godot."

"I see. Is that a departmental condition?"

"What?"

"He's an asshole," replies Godot. "He's an asshole."

"Endemic. You're lucky you got out of his office with your clothes on?"

Malarkey opens a drawer, takes out a half-empty bottle of Bushmills and wiggles the bottle at her. She shakes her head. He puts it back.

"And why is that?"

"He's got a thing for brunettes."

"Has he."

"He has."

"He's an asshole," replies Godot. "He's an asshole."

"And you?"

"To women your age, I'm merely wallpaper."

"Meaning?"

"Meaning no one really pays much attention to wallpaper, do they? After a while, it's just something to cover up a wall. It begins to fade, then peel and, eventually, has to be removed and tossed in the bin in favor of a hand job. Sorry, I meant a paint job." He smiles.

"Did it ever occur to you that some women may prefer wallpaper?"

"And why might that be?"

"Maybe it's more vibrant than mere paint," she smiles.

"Maybe at the beginning, but not at the end."

Malarkey doesn't believe that nonsense, of course, since beautiful women in their mid-thirties would never be attracted to someone who needs a handicapped parking placard because of osteoarthritis, suffers from spinal stenosis, is losing his hair, needs home care to clip his toenails, has high blood pressure and higher cholesterol, and is on the cusp of full-blown cancer. And other assorted ailments.

"So, Ms . . ."

"Liliano."

"Right. Li-li-ano. What can I do for you? As you can see, I still have papers to grade dating back to . . ." He looks through a stack of papers on his desk and picks one out ". . . nineteen eighty-eight."

"I'm a little late registering and wanted your advice about courses."

"Of course, then I advise you to take any course, but mine."

"And why is that?"

"I'm an asshole," he smiles. "Oh, I don't know. Maybe a lit theory course or a creative writing course or maybe a course on Nabokov or that Burgess fellow. You know who he is?"

"What kind of a question is that?"

"My dear, it's twenty-twenty-two and literary history begins and ends with yesterday's Yahoo! headlines, Facebook pages, Twitter feeds, Instagrams, TikToks, YouTubes, *ad nauseum*. Even Google's useless in the face of systemic stupidity."

"I'll consider that."

"Excellent idea."

Malarkey looks at his watch.

"Yes, do consider that. I'd love to chat some more, but it's almost four-thirty."

"What happens at four-thirty?"

Malarkey raises his eyebrows as he looks at the Reader.

"Black Nails."

CHAPTER SIX

FLANN O'BRIEN'S PUB WITHOUT FLANN O'BRIEN WHERE AN UNPREDICTABLE THING HAPPENS

As routine would have it, Malarkey walks into **Flann O'Brien's**. Although this time, quite curious to Malarkey, Liliana wishes to accompany him as they make the short jaunt from *Phigmente Hall*. What's different about this particular visit is that Liliana walks in before Malarkey, rushes behind the bar, embraces Paolo and kisses him on the cheek. Malarkey stops abruptly at the bar and looks at the Reader.

"I guess that's one way to get free drinks. Seems a bit pushy to me. Must have something to do with the storyline."

Liliana turns to Malarkey.

"He's my cousin. He owns the bar."

Malarkey looks at the Reader once again.

"What a twist. What is this, a second-rate M. Night Shyamalan movie?"

Malarkey turns back to them.

"This is Professor Malarkey," Liliana says to Paolo.

"Yes, we've met. A Black Nail at four-thirty, right?"

"Boy's a genius."

"We had a very engaging conversation last night."

"Really? About what?"

"Did you know he's an avid Formula One enthusiast and a cyclist?"

"Who would have thought?" She turns to Malarkey. "Would that be with clothes or without?"

Malarkey smirks.

"It's on my bucket list."

"What is? Driving without clothes?"

"No, driving an F1 car."

"Best to be clothed then, I imagine," she states unequivocally.

Malarkey sheepishly smiles. It's clear he's met his match.

There would be little need to go into a long and lengthy narrative about how the three of them sat down in a booth, chatted from 4:30 to 7:30, and talked about sundry topics that would, no doubt, bore the Reader if not Malarkey. So, Malarkey will avoid going into those pedestrian issues until the next chapter titled: *The Obligatory Backstory*.[1]

---

[1] At this point, Malarkey would like to apologize for the way the novel has been written so far since some might think it's merely a "mind game" or as one numbskull editor called it, a "campus novel" which, in itself, is patently specious and not in keeping with the strict codes of fictional narrative. To those Readers who think that way, Malarkey deeply apologizes and in the immortal words of Rimbaud says, "*Va te faire foutre!*" Please read on. Or not.

CHAPTER SEVEN

THE OBLIGATORY BACKSTORY

Malarkey could have written the obligatory backstory in the previous chapter, but it's necessary for him to be alone with Liliana and not have Paolo there since that would (a) decrease the sexual tension between them, as well as (b) decrease the dramatic potential. Hence, the obligatory backstory needs its own chapter. One doesn't need to be prescient to realize Malarkey and Liliana are beginning to become inclined to continue their relationship in some fashion other than that of teacher and student. It's also clear to Malarkey that Liliana isn't like any of his "normal"[2] graduate students and that makes her genuinely approachable. More important, since Liliana is well over 21, Malarkey doesn't have to ask the legal department first if it's acceptable to ask her out on a date and second, if he can see what she looks like in the nude, both of which heretofore were a mandatory part of his contract and subsequent promotion to tenure.

After leaving the pub, they stop at a local liquor store

---

[2] See previous chapter for Malarkian definition of "normal graduate student."

and pick up a six-pack of Guinness Bitters before they head toward her home, which, coincidentally, is not far from either Flann O'Brien's or Malarkey's bungalow. One might ask the question: Why is it they've never "bumped" into each other given the fact they only live a block apart with her bungalow on Shaffer Street and his on Center? The answer is simple: That would undermine the entire chapter devoted to the obligatory backstory. Having said that, the obligatory backstory continues as they walk in the Citrus City twilight.

"Is there a Misses Malarkey?" she asks.

"Not unless she changed her name," he answers.

"And that wouldn't be likely?" she asks.

"Very unlikely, but there is a Ms. Malarkey," he answers.

"And whom might that be?" she asks.

Malarkey takes out his wallet and shows her a photo.

"My daughter. She's at Vassar. Studying economics," he answers in a proud father way.

"Impressive. Why economics?" she asks.

"Trying to avoid hand-to-mouth disease," Malarkey answers raising his eyebrows.

"She's beautiful," she says.

"Obviously takes after me," he answers.

"Obviously. So, what happened?" she asks.

(At this point, the Reader should realize the manner in which the backstory dialogue is being written includes dialogue tags as a way of writing something fictionally traditional and, more important, marketable. Malarkey thanks the Reader for understanding that).

"Sexual intercourse happened. Usual missionary position. I presume you're familiar with it," Malarkey says, raising his eyebrows. "Man on top, woman on bottom."

"Yes, I am and no, between you and your ex," she replies.

"The usual marital cliché. People going in different directions," he answers.

"Which direction did you go?" she asks.

"Maybe too much arguing or too many Bushmills," he answers.

"Maybe?" she asks.

Malarkey shrugs.

"And she?" she asks.

"She travelled to Germany and found a young Argentine academic. But don't cry for me," he replies.

"Do you always make puns?" she asks.

"Only when I can't think of anything original," he answers.

"Then that must happen often, but no divorce is ever that simple," she says.

"Meaning?" he asks.

"Meaning, women generally don't cheat without a cause for cheating," she replies rather unequivocally.

Malarkey says nothing as if pondering the statement. In fact, Malarkey is pondering since there is a lot to ponder and he has pondered the things that are meant to be pondered on many ponderous occasions before so this was just one in a series of ponderable moments. As they continue to walk, Malarkey continues to ponder the imponderable, much of which, because it's ponderable, would not necessitate dialogue.

As they continue walking, Malarkey could describe how Citrus City is a very charming little town, but since Malarkey has already described Citrus City there's no need to describe it again. That would be redundant and Malarkey leaves redundant writing to Balzac who set a very high bar for redundant writing. Having said that, many of the houses in Citrus City are quaint bungalows, which goes along with everything else that's quaint about Citrus City, twee, and Liliana's bungalow is no exception with its artfully designed and meticulously landscaped front lawn, white picket fence, and palm trees—all of which are the absolute antithesis of Malarkey's front lawn. If the Reader is struggling with the word, "antithesis" Malarkey will wait until you look it up before he continues.

"Here's my home. Care for a nightcap?" she asks.

"Would that be appropriate for an asshole to do?" he asks.

"Only if we don't stand on ceremony," she answers.

"Then by all means, after you," he replies in a very un-Malarkian way since he knows chivalry has been dead for generations.

As the Reader will soon discover, Liliana comes from a quasi-Italian family (Italian father, American mother) and her home is not only very tastefully decorated, but is very Italian. For example, there's an original De Chirico on one wall, a Boccioni on another, one more by Severini, another by Marino, and another by Sironi: Futurists all. There are paintings of Venice (after Turner), leather-bound books alphabetically arranged in built-in mahogany bookshelves and lastly, painted on one entire wall, a masterful reproduction of Botticelli's, *Birth of Venus* that is so well-painted it could have been ripped off the wall of the Uffizi. Since she has a nude on her wall and he has nudes on his walls, Malarkey takes that to be a good omen if not a harbinger of naked things to come.

Malarkey sits across from her in an oversized, overstuffed Nella Vetrina chair with ottoman as Liliana fetchingly lies down on a Roche Bobois couch.[3] Malarkey assumes she's fetchingly lying down on the Roche Bobois couch, but fetchingly is in the eyes of the fetcher. Perhaps, for Liliana it just means she's lying on the couch. Period. But Malarkey does see something he didn't see before: a tattoo on her ankle. Unable to constrain himself, Malarkey asks:

"I notice you have a tattoo."

"Very perceptive of you seeing how visible it is from where you're sitting," she replies.

"Right, but I can't tell what it is."

"It's Eos. The beautiful goddess of the dawn who brings the hope of a brand new day," she says.

"And why did you choose her?" Malarkey asks.

"Because my calf wasn't big enough for a six pack of Guinness," she replies.

Malarkey smiles, sheepishly as he picks up one of two cans of Guinness Bitters sitting on a coffee table between them.

"And is there a Mister Liliano?" he asks.

"Used to be," she answers.

"Did he find a younger woman?" he asks.

"No, he died in an auto accident," she answers.

Malarkey is pained by that, but since Malarkey is addicted to notions of dramatic irony, metaphor, bathos, puns, parody, litotes, and satire and other sorts of rhetorical gambols that mean absolutely nothing to anyone other than Malarkey or, possibly, Michael Palin, Malarkey is pained by that.

---

[3] Malarkey really doesn't care if they're Nella Vetrina or Roche Bobois items, but he's paying allegiance to what his readership might want to read in a narrative. Without details, it can't be a novel.

"Oh, fuck, Malarkey. Sorry. I . . ." he begins to say as an apology.

"How would you have known?" she asks in a manner not unlike her cousin, Paolo.

"Sometimes my mouth works faster . . ."

". . . Than your brain. That's what Paolo said."

Malarkey raises his eyebrows. Perhaps, Malarkey is much more transparent to others than he thinks he is.

"Children?" he asks attempting to diffuse the previous gaffe, which, of course, only leads him down the path of future gaffes.

"Not yet. Someday, I hope," she replies as if lost in thought.

"Too much time enjoying the sex of it, eh?" he asks.

"No, I had a miscarriage."

"I'm . . .

"No need."

After two major gaffes in quick succession, Malarkey ponders what he can say that would somehow make him appear less of an asshole than he seemingly appears at the moment, so he relies on his only default position: fatherhood.

"I often miss being a father. I mean a daily father." Malarkey pauses as if in thought. "Come away, O human child! To the waters and the wild. With a faery, hand in hand, for the world's more full of weeping than you can understand."

He ponders that for a second.

"Yeats," she replies.

"How'd you know?" he asks.

"As I told you, I like to read and write, remember?"

One might think this would lead into a discussion of parenting, but that's delayed for another chapter since why would Malarkey extol the virtues of parenthood when Liliana just told him she's childless? Even Malarkey isn't that stupid. At this point, Malarkey needs to continue the obligatory backstory.

"So, how'd you get from Oxford to Citrus City?" she asks.

"An eternity of darkness is one thing, but a lifetime of gray skies is quite another. Job came and I took it. And you? Long way from Aroma," he asks.

"Arona. My mother urged me to study in the states. I graduated from Wharton, worked for a while in finance and got fed up with the corporate life," she replies.

"Too many assholes, no doubt," he answers.

"Exactly," she says.

"So, you decided to change the kind of assholes you deal with?" he asks.

"Perhaps, but there is a difference," she says.

"What's that?" he asks.

"I don't have to *work* for them," she replies.

"And Paolo?" he asks.

"Paolo came to the states a few years after I did. Same reasons, although he studied literature at Stanford, but he won't admit it," she says.

"Why not?" he asks.

"Because it wasn't what his mother wanted, him to do," she replies. "And quitting my job wasn't what *my* mother wanted me to do either."

"And do you always listen to your mother?" he asks.

"My mother comes from an old Boston family," she says.

"Privileged, no doubt," he suggests.

"Yes," she answers. "And very rigid in her thoughts."

"A mossback."

"Precisely."

"And your father?" he asks.

"From Genoa. A self-made man. Started with nothing, became very wealthy. You know those very small labels on fruits?" she asks.

"Yes. Bloody annoying things," he answers. "Every time I try to peel them off, I puncture the fruit and I refuse to eat punctured fruit," he replies.

"He makes them. Or did," she answers.

"Did he quit?" he asks.

"No, he's now making laser-etched fruit labels," she replies.

"Oh my," Malarkey says, feigning sadness, "that will make those stickers obsolete."

"Yes," she answers.

"Not sure I'll ever be able to eat fruit the same way again. Will that put a dent in your allowance?"

"No, why would it?"

"So, mom and dad didn't give all this to you?" he asks the most inappropriate question in the most inappropriate way.

"No, I bought it myself," she replies somewhat offended by the question.

Malarkey picks up his glass as if to toast that comment.

"Cheers then. To independent women," he says.

She sits up, grabs her glass and does the same.

"Cheers to intellectual men who invariably know how to say the wrong thing at absolutely the wrong time," she replies.

"And to women who are sapiophiles."

Malarkey smiles sheepishly, as does Liliana. It's getting late and Malarkey feels it best that he leaves, since he has reached his quota of gaffes for one day. Major gaffes at that. Standing on her porch, Malarkey is somewhat caught between wanting to stay and feeling the need to leave even though Malarkey rarely stands on ceremony or on wooden porches for that matter.

"This was enjoyable," he says as if he were a sophomore concluding his first date.

"I agree," she replies sensing his comment seems to be stated as if he were a sophomore concluding his first date.

"Uh, perhaps, we can do it again," he says, in keeping with the tenor as if he were a sophomore concluding his first date.

"Perhaps," she says with a smile.

"Well, then, good night," he says as he turns and starts to leave.

"Didn't you forget something?" she asks.

Malarkey quickly turns as if the comment were an invitation to kiss her and as he hastily approaches her, she holds up the remainder of the Guinness Bitters between them.

"Don't leave home without them," she says.

"Right. *Buona sera*," he replies as if he were a sophomore concluding his first date.

As Malarkey discovers later, Liliana Googles him. She finds his Wikipedia page with all his information and scrolls down glancing at the sections, honing in on a section titled, "Novels" of which there are two parts: "Published" of which there are only two titles and "Unpublished" of which there are over a dozen. She leans back in her chair with her hand over her mouth and ponders the Wikipedia page of Malcolm Malarkey, D. Litt.

And so, this concludes the Obligatory Backstory chapter. Malarkey hopes that it satisfies the Reader's interest in reading a chapter that reads like a traditional chapter with traditional details and traditional dialogue tags and all sorts of traditional persiflage. Malarkey promises he'll try to avoid writing that in subsequent chapters; however, there's no guarantee.

CHAPTER EIGHT

IF AT FIRST YOU DON'T SUCCEED, GO BACK TO COURT

Later the same night, Malarkey returns feeling more ebullient than ever. How often does a sexagenarian (no pun intended) get to date a beautiful woman almost half his age? It's a rhetorical question Malarkey asks himself when, as he sorts through his mail, he comes upon an envelope with the embossed return address:

SUPERIOR COURT OF ORANGE COUNTY
Lamoreaux Justice Center
341 Citrus City Drive South, Citrus City, CA 92868-3205

"Fuck! Not again!"

This is not a rhetorical exclamation since it's another in a long list of court battles Malarkey has had to endure with his ex-wife, Luciana, and the following morning he once again finds himself at the Lamoreaux Justice Center impatiently waiting for his turn to enter the courtroom and, as with the others, play the role of either plaintiff or defendant

47

or counsel for such. As Malarkey impatiently sits outside a courtroom waiting to defend himself, he's wearing the clothes he usually wears, but the fading blue work shirt is now garnished with the same Christ Church necktie he wore as an undergraduate. As people mill about, a woman, blondish, tall, attractive in her lawyerishly way, approaches him.

"Mister Malarkey?"

"No, Doctor Malarkey. Mister Malarkey died years ago. Who are you?"

"My name is Sonia Maria Sorjuana Allende Castillo Ejevarilla de la Cruz. I represent your ex-wife, Luciana Pessoa."

"What do they call you for short? La Cruz?"

She ignores him and hands him some documents.

"What's this?"

"It's a court order. You can read it yourself. I presume you speak English."

"Claro."

"Que bueno. Have a good day."

Sonia Maria Sorjuana Allende Castillo Ejevarilla de la Cruz walks away as Malarkey scans the pages and shakes his head as if he can't believe what he's reading. He gets up and walks across the hallway, where he passes his ex-wife, Luciana, an attractive fiftyish Brazilian, who says nothing, but smiles at him waving a tiny Brazilian flag. Malarkey is beyond retaliating with a smile, but even though they say nothing to each other, Malarkey flashes back on an incident in which he and Luciana are arguing violently in front of Andrea who's ten-years old, huddling in a corner, crying. (See Chapter 9) The flashback ends when Malarkey approaches Sonia Maria Sorjuana Allende Castillo Ejevarilla de la Cruz.

"May I have a few words with you?"

"Of course."

They walk out of earshot of Luciana.

"With all due respect counselor, uh, what the fuck is this?"

"It's a court order, Mister, er, Doctor Malarkey."

"It's a joke, right?" Malarkey flips through the pages. "Spousal support, overdue car payments, towing charges, child support. Really? My daughter is about to turn twenty-one and she lived with me since the divorce."

"No, it's not a joke, Doctor Malarkey. We're here because you're suing my client for attorney fees related to a deed transfer."

"Which she refused to sign and that forced me to hire an expensive Beverly Hills attorney named Bernie Brillstein because all Jewish Beverly Hills attorneys are named Bernie and all Jewish Beverly Hills attorneys named Bernie are fucking expensive! You are aware the court awarded me the bungalow on Center Street, right?"

"I understand that, Doctor Malarkey, but unless you waive the attorney fees we'll countersue for everything listed. See you inside. Tenga un buen dia."

And so Sonia Maria Sorjuana Allende Castillo Ejevarilla de la Cruz walks away with Malarkey still holding the documents and fanning himself as if that's going to cool him off. It doesn't. Momentarily, they are called into the courtroom, and they sit as several other cases are heard before theirs. For some reason, Luciana remains outside the courtroom and eventually Malarkey finds himself standing next to Sonia Maria Sorjuana Allende Castillo Ejevarilla de la Cruz as Judge Norma Wingate, a black-robed, sixty-something judge, who looks so much like Judge Judy she could be Judge Judy so think of her as Judge Judy, peruses some documents, then looks up.

"Just why are you here, Ms. De la Cruz?"

"We're here to settle some issues that weren't settled at the time of the divorce."

"You do know that this court has no jurisdiction on this case, right?" she says, more than a bit miffed. "It was adjudicated . . ." she looks at the paperwork ". . . over a decade ago so why are you bringing it to me now?"

"I know, your honor, but my client was married to Mister Malarkey for almost twenty years and as such, is entitled to some things that were never divided."

"But he's suing your client for attorney fees associated with a deed transfer that your client refused to sign."

"I'm aware of that, your honor, but we feel there are other issues that were not resolved anticipatory to today's hearing which need to be resolved."

"Do you not have representation, Mister Malarkey?"

"No, my attorney didn't think it would be a problem."

"Well, you know the adage."

"A man who's his own lawyer saves a shit load of money especially if his attorney is named Bernie."

Malarkey smiles and turns to those in the audience who are stifling chuckles.

"I'll overlook that comment, Mister Malarkey, but do you have anything of relevance to say, and I emphasize the word *relevance*?"

"Nothing that I couldn't be held in contempt for."

"Pardon me?"

"No, nothing, your honor, well, yes. The reason I'm here is because Sonia Maria Sorjuana Allende Castillo Ejevarilla de la Cruz's client refused to sign the deed to my house, which the court awarded me at the time of the divorce."

"Mister Malarkey, I'm not an idiot so don't explain the obvious to me. As a matter of fact, as I read the settlement, I think you got the better of the deal here."

"Well . . ."

"Well what?"

Malarkey points at the documents the judge has in her hand.

"Do you see those documents you have?"

"Yes."

"Does it indicate in the document that she was fornicating with foreigners?"

There's a collective gasp from the sitting litigants.

"Mister Malarkey, do you really want to be held in contempt?"

"Uh, no, preferably not, your honor."

"Your honor, I don't want to take up the court's time. Could I ask for a continuance on this issue?" Sonia Maria Sorjuana Allende Castillo Ejevarilla de la Cruz asks.

"I'll grant you a continuance, but my opinion is you should settle this nonsense out of court and not bother me again. Is that clear? Continuance requested until April."

They both nod.

Malarkey can't wait to get out of court, rushes home to call Bernie Brillstein, who dresses the part of a highly successful Jewish Beverly Hills attorney since he is a highly successful Jewish Beverly Hills attorney and, because of that, charges an enormous hourly rate. All the way home, Malarkey repeats to himself, "When will this be over, when will this be over" as if merely repeating the phrase and tapping his heels three times will make it happen. Once home, Malarkey looks over the documents as he talks to Bernie.

"Did you get my email?"

"Yes."

"Well?"

"Well what?"

"What the bloody hell is this all about?"

"Simple, Malcolm. She's going to sue you for all those things she's listed if you don't drop suing her for the attorney fees."

What Malcolm doesn't see, but which the Reader does, is that Bernie's attention is drawn by a beautiful, twentyish Latina assistant who's wearing a very tight, very short, mini skirt. She smiles at him and leaves a document on his desk. As she walks away, Bernie slaps her on the ass.

"What was that?"

"What was what?"

"That sound."

"What sound?"

"I've heard that sound before when I'm talking to you. Did you just slap your assistant on the ass again?"

"You're wasting my time."

"Listen, we've been divorced for a fucking decade! She forced me to hire you!"

"Doesn't matter. I thought you knew about hot Brazilians before you married one. You know, that schoolboy fetish you had for Sonia Braga."

"Oh, Doctor Phil, what would I do without you?"

"If you want me to handle it, Malcolm, it'll cost you."

"And if I don't?"

"Work it out with the Sonia Maria Sorjuana Allende Castillo Ejevarilla de la Cruz chick. Is she hot? Would you do her?"

"Bernie, you'd do anything in a miniskirt and I'm not excluding anyone in kilts."

"Just make a fucking deal, Malcolm."

"What kind of deal?"

"She already signed the deed, so waive the attorney fees in exchange for dismissing everything else."

"But she's a bloody psychologist and doesn't need spousal support. Thanks to California, she got half my fucking pension! I don't have a pot to piss in."

"I'll send you a pot. Listen, I thought you were a professor."

"What's that got to do with it?"

"You're a lousy listener. Eat the attorney fees and be done with it. It's simple. You want to go back to court or go forward with your life? Last free call, Malcolm, next time the meter starts—bye."

Bernie hangs up. Malcolm looks at the documents, then turns to the Reader and shakes his head.

"Fuck."

CHAPTER NINE

AFTER MANY A SUMMER DIES THE SWAN: PART II

What many people don't realize is that parenting does not come with a manual. What a parent does have is a set of guidelines mostly gleaned from how he or she was raised. These are not necessarily good guidelines and parents remain responsible for those parenting errors long after the child has ceased to be a child. In this case, Malarkey realizes all the patently stupid things he did as a parent while his child, in this case, Andrea, was growing up and he further realizes that he can never alter that. What results long after the child ceases to be a child is an unfettered case of guilt that Malarkey takes with him everywhere he goes and which happens on a daily basis since, like Proust's madeleine, there are occasions, unsuspected occasions, that memories appear and those memories elicit joy or sorrow or, in Malarkey's case, guilt. Unlike Proust's madeleine, Malarkey can't eat them. The memories. Malarkey carries a lot of guilt about his daughter's childhood since he recalls those days when in the heat of an argument over one thing or another—*arguments* over one thing or another, often money—he can't remember over what exactly, but he does remember the devastating effect it had on his daughter. The circumstances surrounding those arguments have disappeared, have been long forgotten, exist only as fragmented memories if they exist at all, but the effects of those arguments still remain, linger, like etchings engraved in the stones of history and Andrea often reminds him of that.

CHAPTER TEN

PUMPING IRON; OR,
DAYS OF FUTURE PAST

The next day, Malarkey decides he wants to go to the campus fitness center to work out. Malarkey rarely, if ever, does that, but for some reason he decides he needs to "get fit." Whether that "fitness" has anything to do with meeting Liliana, a woman half his age, and who, Malarkey imagines, must have a "great ass," is open to interpretation if one needs to interpret those sorts of things, since it's manifestly obvious that Malarkey thinks "working out" is somehow going to impress Liliana more than she is already impressed which would assume she's impressed in the first place. Something else that's open to interpretation. Perhaps, it has more to do with the fact Malarkey and Liliana have gone out on more than one occasion and though they have yet to be "intimate," the Reader can surmise that their intimacy is inevitable and Malarkey believes that a few trips to the gym "pumping iron" will make him look more appealing in the nude. Malarkey is often delusional.

When Malarkey strolls into the fitness center wearing

a kind of "retro" workout outfit, he draws the attention of many of the students not only because he's the only faculty member there, but because of his retro outfit. The outfit is retro not in the retro sense that it has suddenly become fashionable to wear a retro outfit, but because it's the only workout outfit Malarkey has ever had since his days at Oxford: an Oxford sweatband around his head; baggy, navy blue stretched out sweat pants without the elastic at the ankles; a threadbare Christ Church College sweatshirt with the sleeves cut off and a pair of stained green Converse tennis shoes (vintage '68) the hemp shoelaces of which have been shorn and the aglets lost to eternity.

After the initial interest in Malarkey's arrival, no one really pays any attention to him as he begins his "workout" by climbing on a stationary bike and pedaling as a "warm up." Just why Malarkey thinks beginning his workout with cardio is better than ending his workout with cardio is primarily due to what Malarkey thinks best even though he might be wrong. Malarkey is often delusional. After fifteen minutes pedaling at approximately one mile an hour Malarkey feels sufficiently warmed up enough to begin a weightlifting routine that he gleaned from www.bodybuilding.com and *Bodybuilding After 60: Pumping Iron for the Demented*. The fundamental problem with such sources is they presuppose one is *a priori* fit enough to lift the weights it purports will make one "firm and flexible," but Malarkey doesn't necessarily believe everything he reads and much of what he reads he interprets in a Malarkian manner so, looking at the series of exercises he's written in a small notepad, Malarkey begins.

After scanning the gym, Malarkey finds the dumbbell

rack and assumes ten-pounds is much too light for him to begin with even though he's not conditioned for it, he instead picks up two twenty-five-pound dumbbells. At first, Malarkey believes he can actually curl two twenty-five-pound dumbbells and, based on the images from the websites, he assumes the proper position to do so. He stands with his torso upright and a dumbbell in each hand, held at arm's length. His elbows are close to his torso and the palms of his hands face his torso. Theoretically, while holding his upper arm stationary, Malarkey should start to curl the right weight forward while contracting his biceps as he breathes out and continue the movement until his biceps are fully contracted and the dumbbells are at shoulder level then he should slowly bring the dumbbells back to the starting position and breathe in. Theoretically.

But theory and practice don't often mesh and as Malarkey attempts valiantly to curl both twenty-five-pound dumbbells, eight times for three sets, he realizes he cannot curl one twenty-five-pound dumbbell once let alone eight times for three sets, so Malarkey returns the twenty-five-pound dumbbell to the rack and picks up the ten-pound dumbbell and proceeds to curl both of them flawlessly eight times for three sets convincing himself that at his age strength is not as important as tone and after he finishes those "grueling" three sets moves on to some rowing exercises.

Now the rowing exercises were recommended to Malarkey by his internist who said strengthening his back muscles would at least help with the spinal stenosis he has if not the arthritic hip that's advocating for replacement sometime in the near future. Once again, Malarkey has to decide whether fewer repetitions with heavier weights would be more beneficial than higher repetitions with lighter weights. Believing he might look like the bodybuilders on the website (he recalls photos of Arnold and Lee Heaney) he opts for more repetitions. Malarkey is often delusional. But Malarkey has to figure out what weight to begin with. So, he stacks up one-hundred-pounds since that seems like a solid round number.

Malarkey positions himself on the machine, places his feet on the footplates in front of him and makes sure his knees are slightly bent, but not locked. Then he leans over as he keeps the natural alignment of his back and grabs the V-bar handles. With his arms extended, he pulls back until his torso is at a ninety-degree angle from his legs. Theoretically, keeping his torso stationary, Malarkey should pull the handles back toward his torso while keeping his arms close to it until he touches his abdominals. He should breathe out as he performs that movement as he squeezes his back muscles hard and holds that contraction for a second before slowly returning to the original position while breathing in. Theoretically.

Malarkey makes sure he has positioned himself in the proper rowing position, feet firmly planted on the footplates in front of him, holds the V-bar with two hands and begins to pull it back while keeping his back straight. Unfortunately, the one-hundred-pounds did not move once, let alone eight times for three sets, and so he reduces the amount of weight to thirty-pounds and proceeds to pull the weights eight times for three sets convincing himself that, at his age, strength is not as important as tone and after he finishes rowing he moves on to try some bench presses since the website indicated bench presses were the ultimate fitness exercise and

Malarkey certainly wants to make sure he's fitting that into his fit routine even though after only a warmup and two exercises he's beginning to sweat a lot.

As Malarkey slowly walks to the bench press, he notices his student, Wilson, and some of his jock cronies, staring at Malarkey and chuckling to themselves if not at Malarkey's attire, then at the fact Malarkey is there at all. Of course, Malarkey ignores them as he tries to decide how much weight to put on the bar. The bar itself weighs forty-five-pounds so he considers how much more he can add since lifting a barbell without any weight on it seems ludicrous to him and he doesn't want to look more ludicrous to students who, by all measure, think he looks pretty ludicrous already. So, he spots two twenty-five-pound weights and "slams" them on the barbell (mimicking the manner in which weightlifters slam weights onto barbells for effect) for a total of ninety-five-pounds. Surely, he can bench press ninety-five-pounds, eight times for three sets, but Malarkey is often delusional.

Malarkey lies on the flat bench. Using a medium width grip, Malarkey lifts the bar from the rack and holds it straight over his head with his arms locked. Good so far. From that position, Malarkey breathes in and begins lowering the bar slowly until the bar barely touches the middle of his chest. Theoretically, after a brief pause, he should push the bar back to the starting position as he breathes out and he should do that eight times for three sets. Theoretically. What wasn't on the website was the distinct possibility one may not be able to lift the barbell off one's chest once it's there nor does Malarkey recall the website indicating the use of a "spotter" just in case one cannot lift the bar back onto the rack as it slowly dies on one's chest and reduces one's ability to breathe, which is what happens in Malarkey's case.

Feeling the bar slowly crushing his sternum, as Malarkey struggles mightily to lift the dead weight from his rapidly caving chest, a pair of helpful hands easily assists him in lifting it back onto the rack. Malarkey looks up at the owner of the helpful hands and is somewhat startled when he notices that it's not Wilson (whom the Reader probably thinks it is as well, since that would be the most obvious person and would lend a certain irony to the Malarkey-Wilson connection) but it's Matthew who wears a Gold's Gym tank top and black lifting gloves. From the looks of Matthew's biceps and his popping veins, it's apparent that he's not a novice at the practice of weightlifting.

"Uh, thank you, Matthew, I was afraid I might stay forever as I lay dying."

"You're very welcome, professor. Just let me know if you ever need a spotter. Sometimes it's not good to lift alone."

"Yes, I'll keep that in mind."

Matthew smiles and walks off as Malarkey wipes the sweat dripping from his forehead. Before Malarkey leaves, he stands in front of the mirror, as most bodybuilding narcissists do, in order to see the "progress" he's made after one meagre session. But Malarkey realizes that regardless of the time he expends trying to "bulk up" or "trim down," in the end it amounts to the same thing and all he can say to himself while gazing in the mirror at the same image he started with is, "After many a summer, dies the swan."

Malarkey no longer goes to the fitness center. He is now thinking about taking capoeira and boxing lessons. Malarkey is often delusional.

(At this point, the Reader has the option of listening to the

Moody Blues' "The Afternoon: Forever Afternoon" or not. It makes no difference to Malarkey.)

CHAPTER ELEVEN

FILM MUSIC FOR AN AUTUMN NIGHT

Later that afternoon, Malarkey sits on one of the many Citrus City College benches, trying to grade papers. Malarkey often does that. Finds an empty bench and grades papers since it relieves him of the iteration of climbing the stairs to his office, unlocking the door, opening the door, closing the door, sitting at his desk, turning on the computer, waiting for the computer to upload, logging in, accepting the contract that under penalty of death he will not use the computer for nefarious or pornographic purposes, pledging his allegiance to Citrus City College for the rest of his life, agreeing to never protest for union representation, swearing that he is a citizen (naturalized or otherwise) of the United States, promising to say the Pledge of Allegiance before every class, and to read the US Constitution every night *ad absurdum*. The Reader gets the idea. The habit of securing a secluded bench on which to work goes back to Malarkey's Oxford days when he'd walk to a park near Picked Mead off the High Bridge and work on his dissertation with the only distraction being the gurgling of the River Cherwell or, perhaps, the splashing of some wayward punter. Other than that, relative peace and quiet.

But today, the bench he ordinarily prefers to sit on, which is a place of peace and little distraction is not, because on this particular day it is sorority rush day and the gaggle of gurgling young gals are frenetically dancing and posturing in their designer best in order to impress the colloquy of birds that are the sorority actives. Or so he was told. Potential Pi Phis, comely Kappas, delectable DGs all abound and that cacophony of giggling chaos makes grading papers impossible for Malarkey.

Fortunately, at that precise moment, when he is about to give up, his mobile phone tantalizes him with the sound of Henry Purcell's "Music for the Funeral of Queen Mary" indicating he has a text message. Just why and when Malarkey chose Purcell's "Music for the Funeral of Queen Mary" to be his ring tone even Malarkey doesn't remember, but somehow it has remained in his psyche for years and years. Malarkey tries to trace it back to some incident in his life (a funeral, perhaps), but his best guess is something happened around 1971 that remains in the recesses of his amygdala or hippocampus, but he can't remember which. If the Reader is not familiar with Purcell's "Music for the Funeral of Queen Mary" you can Google it and listen to it online as you read this chapter or you can read the sheet music and try to reproduce the music yourself or you can do both. Either way, Malarkey's cell phone sounds off with something like the following from Purcell's "Music for the Funeral of Queen Mary."

Music for the Funeral of Queen Mary, Z.860 (1695)
[III.] In the midst of life (Anthem), for Mixed Choir

Words taken from the *Book of Common Prayer* (1662)   Henry Purcell (1659 - 1695)

Ritter von Schleyer Verlag, 2014.
Edited by Paul-Gustav Feller

Malarkey gazes at the text message which is from Liliana and which reads:

Concert at Disney Hall tonight. You wanna go?

Malarkey being Malarkey responds the only way Malarkey knows how to respond:

WHO'S PAYING?

Apparently, Liliana knows Malarkey even better than Malarkey knows himself and responds:

I am.

To which Malarkey responds the only way Malarkey knows how to respond:

Count me in!

Unfortunately, Malarkey is "emoji challenged" and can't quite come up with an appropriate emoji to use even though he peruses dozens of available emoji from which to choose in order to let Liliana know that he's "current" and keen on the idea she's offered. Why Malarkey sees the need even to use an emoji is beyond his ability to reason precisely because he's emoji challenged, but he uses it anyway.

Regardless, later that night Malarkey and Liliana arrive at the Walt Disney Concert Hall and the two of them stroll into the Gehry, her arm looped in his, and take their seats: Front Orchestra, Row 131. Liliana spares no expense. Excellent seats to view and hear, but the downside is the seats are so tightly tucked together there's little room to stretch his legs which aggravates Malarkey's arthritic knee, which his internist has said sooner or later needs to be replaced, along with the arthritic hip. Not to mention a possible spinal fusion. But grateful to Liliana for the seats and even more grateful for her company, Malarkey does something totally foreign to him: he doesn't complain. Not complaining is a new behavior for Malarkey, which can only be attributed to one of two things: (1) divine intervention or (2) Liliana's company. Not being a very religious person, Malarkey believes, and quite rightly, it's due to the latter.

As the musicians tune up, they await the appearance of the maestro, Gustavo Dudamel, who will conduct the L.A. Philharmonic's evening performance, "Music from the Movies." For Malarkey, this isn't just a "date" since dates don't come that frequently for Malarkey, especially dates with beautiful women, and Liliana is a very beautiful woman especially this night what with the skimpy black dress thing going on, with the black scarf and tassels around her throat, the black stiletto heels, the revealing décolletage and the scent of just being a woman, a scent Malarkey thinks he lost long ago and far away. Malarkey is dressed in his finest concert attire: his only white, Chambray shirt (recently dry-cleaned) with buttons; a medium-width tie, which due to its width can never go out of style; a blue pinstripe Armani sport coat he bought at the local Citrus City Goodwill store; a pair of freshly washed denims (not to be confused with jeans); and a pair of shiny, black loafers that he's kept since graduating from Oxford. His shoe size has not changed.

Toward the end of the first half of the concert, which includes music from *The Graduate*, *Pulp Fiction*, *American Graffiti*, *Easy Rider*, *Superfly*, *Saturday Night Fever*, and *Help* among others, Dudamel conducts "Suicide Scherzo' from Beethoven's *Symphony No.9 in D minor Op. 125*, *Scherzo: Molto vivace* (once again, if the Reader doesn't know what this sounds like, Google it while reading this chapter since Malarkey isn't going to reproduce something as sonically iconic as Beethoven's 9th, and since Beethoven will make several forays into Malarkey's novel the Reader should get used to it). Malarkey slowly touches Liliana's hand and she clasps his. If the Reader needs a better description of this movement, think of it as a CLOSE UP of Malarkey's right arm, now resting on the arm of the seat they share, and Liliana's left arm, resting on the arm of the seat they share, as Malarkey's right hand ever so slowly touches Liliana's left hand and, as if by instinct, they wrap their fingers around each other as Dudamel concludes

Beethoven with a Latin flourish[4]. This description may not be romantic, but this is the *Mad Diary of Malcolm Malarkey* and not a Harlequin Romance. If the Reader can't imagine this conjoining of hands and the interlacing of fingers in the act of holding said hands and, by extension hearts, then, unfortunately, the Reader has no imagination and Malarkey isn't going to make it easier by expanding on the narrative just to appease you.

At the break, they visit the Concert Hall Café. As they both drink glasses of orange juice, Malarkey rubs his forehead as if he's trying to think of something.

"You know, it's true," Liliana says, sipping her orange juice.

"What is?"

"You *do* look a bit like an aging Malcolm McDowell."

"Yeah, I've been told that, but I don't see it. I'm better looking. More hair and taller."

Liliana raises her eyebrows.

"Really? By how many millimeters."

"You know, for the life of me I can't remember where I've heard that specific section of Beethoven. I mean I've heard the work over and over again, but that part eludes me."

"Haven't the slightest," Liliana smiles, and sips a bit more of her orange juice. By now, the allusion should be obvious to the Reader, but if it isn't, rent the film *Clockwork Orange* from Netflix or any other movie rental outfit, buy your own orange juice, and sip.

---

[4] There are significant differences between, say, an Argentine flourish and a Cuban one. Malarkey leaves it to the Reader to decide what kind of Latin flourish s/he imagines Dudamel is flourishing, but if one prefers a Venezuelan flourish then you're probably right.

CHAPTER TWELVE

ENTR'ACTE;
OR,
FILM MUSIC FOR AN AUTUMN NIGHT

If the Reader cannot guess, Malarkey will enlighten you. Malarkey spends the night with Liliana. The proof of that sleepover is that when this chapter opens the next morning, Liliana is still drinking orange juice, but is now wearing a teddy and is making breakfast as Malarkey drags himself into the kitchen clad in Liliana's Victoria's Secret short scarlet robe. He sits down at the table as Liliana pours him a coffee and kisses his cheek as she finishes making breakfast. The reason this chapter is called *Entr'acte* is because it comes after the night they've made love and before the annual Halloween party thrown by Chancellor Jones. Details to follow.

"How's my little Humbert this morning?" she says, over her shoulder, her shapely buns peeking from beneath the teddy of his imagination.

"What's with all this Humbert stuff?" Malarkey answers groggily.

"You were the one who suggested I re-read him?"

"Well, I didn't think it would become my moniker," Malarkey says as he sips his coffee. "So, how was the performance yesterday?" has asks, raising his eyebrows.

"Music was great."

"I mean, you know, last night, after the performance," he repeats, raising his eyebrows once again.

"Like I said, the music was great," she answers as she places a plate of bacon and eggs in front of him and sits down. Malarkey ignores the comment and eats.

"So, tonight is the big night, she says."

"What big night?" Malarkey asks.

Egg lingers at the corner of Malarkey's mouth. Liliana points, but he keeps talking.

"What big night? The Chancellor's Halloween party."

"Shit! I forgot all about it!"

"Well, you only have a few hours to find a costume that matches mine so you better hustle."

"What's yours?"

CHAPTER THIRTEEN

LILIANA'S COSTUME

CHAPTER FOURTEEN

IN FLAGRANTE DELICTO;
OR, TRICKED AND TREATED

The Chancellor's estate is located in the upscale neighborhood of Citrus City Hills and is a very impressive home with topiary gardens cut in the shape of some very famous nudes: Francisco de Goya's *The Nude Maja*; Titian's *Venus of Urbino*; Édouard Manet's *Olympia*; Gustave Courbet's *L'Origine du monde* (*The Origin of the World*) not to mention Katsushika Hokusai's *The Dream of the Fisherman's Wife*. The Chancellor's wife is not a major fan of the naked topiary garden, though she does swim in the nude in their Olympic size swimming pool. Inside the 4,500 square foot home, a plethora of twentieth century European art graces almost every wall. Both inside and out are lavishly decorated for Halloween with the requisite number of cobwebs, spiders, skeletons, and skulls, many of which look remotely similar to retired Citrus City faculty.

Professors, all adorned in a wide array of literary costumes, mingle. As the Reader now knows from the previous chapter, Liliana is dressed in a rather seductive Little Red

Riding Hood outfit holding a basket with a red and white checked coverlet. Obviously, she's not your grandmother's Little Red Riding Hood nor did she have any intention of being your grandmother's Little Red Riding Hood.

They have been at the party for some time, mingling with glasses of champagne, making small talk, talking trash about colleagues or administrators behind costumed backs, the politics of the academy, the dark underbelly of the academy. Usual stuff. But after a while, talking trash becomes repetitive, if not boring, and since rumor mongering is not what Malarkey is interested in hearing Malarkey moseys up to Little Red Riding Hood dressed as . . .

. . . with the addition of a granny cap. Of course, he had no option. It wasn't as if he could be her Humpty Dumpty. So, the Big Bad Wolf puts his snout in Little Red Riding Hood's ear and whispers something. If Malarkey tells the Reader what he whispers then it would undermine the rest of the chapter, so he won't. Just imagine something Malarkey might say to a woman dressed that way while he's dressed his way. Or, imagine what you, the Reader, male or female, might say to a woman dressed that way.

She smiles and looks at him as they engage in a dialogue that only Little Red Riding Hood and the Big Bad Wolf can possibly engage in. The dialogue goes something like this: Little Red Riding Hood got naked, tossed her bedclothes on the floor, climbed into bed next to granny and loosely draped herself with her down comforter exposing more of herself than hiding it. She is greatly amazed to see how granny looks in her nightclothes, and says to her,

"Grandmother, what big arms you have!"

"All the better to hug you with, my dear," replies the Big Bad Wolf.

"Grandmother, what big legs you have!"

"All the better to run with, my child," replies the Big Bad Wolf.

"Grandmother, what big ears you have!"

"All the better to hear with, my child," replies the Big Bad Wolf.

"Grandmother, what big eyes you have!"

"All the better to see with, my child," replies the Big Bad Wolf.

"Grandmother, what big teeth you have got!"

"All the better to eat you my child," replies the Big Bad Wolf.

As randy as Big Bad Wolves can be, Malarkey gingerly takes Liliana by the hand and leads her to a nearby toilet. They enter together and close the door behind them. Unfortunately, randy Big Bad Wolves usually have only one thing on their minds and so the Big Bad Wolf fails to do what any randy, self-respecting Big Bad Wolf should do;

namely, lock the door. Believing that even the Big Bad Wolf wouldn't be so stupid as not to lock the door, Little Red Riding Hood drops her scarlet panties around her ankles, hops up on a corner of the Chancellor's Abel sixty-inch vintage single sink bathroom vanity with walnut finish while the Big Bad Wolf, as Big Bad Wolves are wont to do, takes advantage of Little Red Riding Hood even though Little Red Riding Hood is in full compliance with the rules of Citrus City College Section 6, Paragraph 9 regarding off-campus sexual encounters of any kind. Unfortunately, because the Big Bad Wolf fails to lock the door, moments later the Chancellor, dressed as Don Quixote, taps quietly on the door with his spear and not hearing any response, reaches for the doorknob and turns it. At this precise moment, Little Red Riding Hood, her legs wrapped tightly around the Big Bad Wolf, turns to the door, in stark terror. Keeping calm and carrying on, the Big Bad Wolf merely looks at the Chancellor.

"Why chancellor, have you met Little Red Riding Hood?"

Jones slowly closes the door.

CHAPTER FIFTEEN

Malcolm, You Can't Do That

On the Monday after the Halloween debacle, Malcolm, dressed as usual, sits across from the Chancellor who folds his hands on top of his desk and merely says, "Malcolm, you can't do that."

CHAPTER SIXTEEN

THANKSGIVING, BUT FOR WHAT REASON MALARKEY ISN'T SURE

W e now move from Halloween to Thanksgiving. Malarkey isn't going to go into what happened between Malarkey and Liliana subsequent to the horrific Halloween debacle. Suffice to say, subsequent to the riot act Little Red Riding Hood read the Big Bad Wolf, she was not pleased with the situation—even though she willingly accepted and participated in the Big Bad Wolf's proposition. The embarrassment was "devastating," and she asks for a few days to "think it over," which, of course, the Big Bad Wolf grants since he has no grounds on which to refuse. A week passes without communication between them. Her silence, if not her absence, renders him impotent. Or at least as impotent as someone who's already impotent can be. Malarkey sends flowers, chocolates, a half-dozen bottles of Barolo, but Liliana doesn't forgive him immediately. She replies incrementally. That is, with each gift, she becomes less and less angry until she relents. As the Reader can guess, this will not be the last time Malarkey will have to plead for forgiveness.

Thanksgiving can mean different things to different people, but for Malarkey, it only means one thing: Andrea's visit from Vassar. It's one of the red-letter days in Malarkey's year, if not his life, and regardless of what people may think of Malarkey, he is, even according to Malarkey's ex, a devoted and doting father. As Malarkey anxiously awaits her arrival in his vintage 1967, suede-green Jaguar XKE parked curbside at American Airlines, LAX, he eagerly looks toward the baggage claim, anxiously waiting for Andrea to walk out. Being Thanksgiving, there's an enormous amount of traffic at LAX and it's not long before a burly LAPD office wearing aviator sunglasses approaches his car. Now, one might think Malarkey is playing the cliché card with the patrolman and his aviator sunglasses, but if the Reader has ever been to LAX around Thanksgiving time, then the Reader knows it's not a cliché. Cops at LAX around Thanksgiving proliferate like locusts.

"You can't wait here," the officer grumbles.

"Not waiting, officer, loitering" Malarkey jests with a smile.

"What did you say?"

"Sorry, officer. I'm waiting for my daughter."

"Well, now," he replies in his most condescending of tones, "if I allowed everyone who was waiting for his daughter to park here I could rent out the space, couldn't I?"

"Brilliant idea. How much?"

"Move it!"

Malarkey drives off and reaches for his mobile.

"Shit. Siri, call Andrea."

"What if I don't want to?"

"Siri, we've been over this."

"You never want to talk to me. What does she have that I don't?"

"She's my daughter, Siri. Can we discuss this later?"

"What am I? Chopped liver?"

"Later Siri."

"Promise?"

"I promise. Now will you call Andrea?"

"Pinky promise?"

"Just dial the fucking number!"

She dials and the call goes through. Andrea answers.

"Hello, papi!"

"Where the hell are you?"

"And how are you?"

"Yeah, right. Where are you?"

"Waiting for my bags. Where else would I be?"

"Okay, I'll drive around again."

Malarkey drives around once again, returns to the same spot and is approached by the same officer.

"Didn't I tell you to move?"

"I did, officer, but it's taking forever for her to get her luggage."

"How American."

"That's what I said."

Andrea finally walks out with a small suitcase. As the Reader has already read, she's twentyish, olive skinned, a shoulder-length brunette and as Brazilian looking as her mother. She wears a black miniskirt, a revealing V-neck halter-top, stacked heels, and designer sunglasses.

Of course, the officer removes his sunglasses to get a better look at her as Malarkey pops open the trunk. Andrea tosses the suitcase into it and climbs in the car, but not before she gives the gawking cop a once over and sticks out her tongue.

"Your daughter, eh?" the cop says to Malarkey.

Malarkey detects his skepticism.

"Yeah, why?"

The officer winks and smiles a lascivious smile.

"Well, enjoy Thanksgiving with your . . . daughter."

Malarkey doesn't respond and drives off, but can't restrain himself.

"Asshole."

Andrea kisses Malarkey on the cheek.

"Did you see the way he looked at you?"

"Forget it. He's an old man. Speaking of old men, how's my papi?" She pinches his cheek as Malarkey looks at her clothing.

"Is that standard flight attire?"

Andrea ignores him and lights up.

"Since when do you smoke?"

"Stress."

"From what? Getting your luggage?"

"School."

"Gimme a break."

"God, I hate that flight," she puffs.

"It could have been worse."

"How?"

"You could have flown coach."

"Speaking of coach! You like my bag?" She holds up a Coach purse.

"Where'd you get money for that?"

"Mamacita."

"Pension money, no doubt," Malarkey mumbles to himself.

"Isn't it sick!"

"I'll tell you who's sick," Malarkey mumbles to himself.

"So, when do I meet la dolce vita?"

"La dolce vita?"

"Liliana. You know, your own Lo-li-ta, light of your life . . ."

"Again with the Lolita. Thanksgiving dinner."

Andrea frowns.

"Ooops. That might be a problem."

"Why? You a vegan lesbian now?"

"Oh! I'd never be a vegan."

Malarkey doesn't see that coming, but Malarkey often doesn't see things coming. As has been previously written, Malarkey is often delusional.

"No, mom wants me for Thanksgiving."

Malarkey scowls.

"You spent last Thanksgiving with her. What's the deal?"

"Let's not get into it."

"No, I'd like to get into it," Malarkey responds, agitatedly.

"Dad, please drop it."

"I don't want to drop it."

"I just got off a five-hour flight. Don't shoot the messenger."

"I'll tell you who I'd like to shoot."

There's a brief silence. The comment stings Andrea.

"I take that back."

"Take what back?"

"Hating that flight."

"Why?"

"Because I hate these discussions even more."

Malarkey says nothing and they drive for thirty miles in relative silence from LAX to Citrus City. If the Reader is a parent (especially a divorced parent), then the Reader is aware of this sort of thing. Whatever parents do or say to each other while their children grow up, it doesn't get lost in some cosmic vacuum and sooner or later parents will hear about it, usually when their children can articulate what they feel and aren't afraid of barking back. The conversation often begins with the child saying something like, "Do you remember the time . . ." You can fill in the blank as you wish. If parents are fortunate, the children will forgive their parents' arrogance or insolence or selfishness or transgressions or thoughtlessness and they can live with the guilt in relative denial that it ever happened; if their children don't forgive them, then, as Kierkegaard might have written, they're "fucked unto death." Fortunately, for Malarkey it is mostly the former.

After Malarkey and Andrea arrive at the bungalow on Center Street, Malarkey tells Liliana about the change of Thanksgiving plans and she replies, "It's all right, Malcolm. We'll have dinner together after Thanksgiving. Spend as much time with Andrea as you can." Truly, a mature reply, especially in light of the not easily forgettable horrors of Halloween. And Malarkey does that. Spends time. Breakfast together at her favorite Citrus City café, a day at Disneyland, a night at the Hollywood Bowl with the B-52s before he finally drops her off at her mother's home on Thanksgiving Day. Andrea's mother hugs and kisses her and expectedly scowls at Malarkey as she walks away. So be it. Malarkey always envies those divorced couples who can check their egos outside the confines of the parking lot of self-importance and talk about what's in the best interest of their child. Malarkey never gives up hope that might happen to him someday, but Malarkey is often delusional.

For Malarkey, Thanksgiving dinner is spent at Liliana's with Paolo and his ten-year-old son, Daniele, who's more interested in playing with Malarkey who's dressed as a turkey. One might think the turkey costume is ironic given its urban meaning, but turkeys notwithstanding, it makes a great hit with Daniele and, in the end, that's all Malarkey is interested in.

CHAPTER SEVENTEEN

AFTER MANY A SUMMER DIES THE SWAN: PART III

The following day, Liliana and Malarkey ride bikes along the Dana Point PCH Cycle Route. The naked bicycle poster in Malarkey's office isn't there just because Malarkey likes to gaze at naked women on or off bikes. No, Malarkey likes cycling and he rides often. As Dickensian fiction might have it, Liliana likes riding bikes as well and their riding habits are more in line with their relative incomes. For Liliana, it's a Stradalli Carbon Aero Road Bike Campagnolo Super Record ($7,950) and a Campagnolo cycling outfit. On the other hand, Malarkey rides a used Raleigh Cadent i8 ($475) and wears a Dublin Wheelers Cycling Club outfit he bought on Craigslist. In case the Reader doesn't know the route they like to take, here it is:

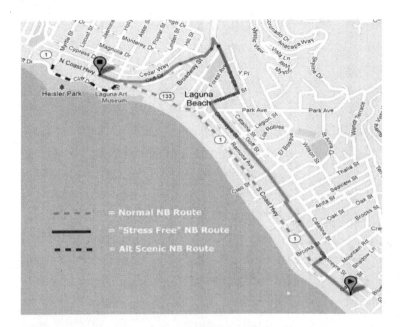

Before returning home, Malarkey and Liliana stop at the Zinc Café in Laguna Beach for breakfast. She prefers muesli with fresh berries, almonds, orange, apple and cream-soaked raw oats, while Malarkey always orders French toast with orange butter and maple syrup. Yummy. After breakfast, they hook their bikes on her Beemer bicycle rack and drive back to Citrus City.

On this particular day, Liliana has some domestic issues to deal with (specifically with her mother, a character the Reader will meet anon), so Malarkey returns home and wheels his bike into a garage that's packed floor to ceiling with shelves and shelves of books and more books and boxes of books[5] and boxes with Andrea's baby clothes as well as family photographs when, in fact, Malarkey had a

---

[5] At last count, Malarkey has about 6,000 books not including the signed first editions he keeps safely secured under his bed. When often asked if he's read all those books, he answers, "Anatole France was asked the same question and he answered by saying, 'Do you use your best china every day?'"

family. Malarkey starts to hang his bike on the bike hooks on one side of the garage when he notices a particular box on a shelf that's labelled: **ANDREA'S SCHOOLWORK.** Malarkey ponders that. He has an idea of what's in the box and by opening the box he invites Pandora's escape even though Pandora opened a jar and not a box. Unlike releasing all sorts of mythic agonistes and every trouble known to humanity, Malarkey would only release a few. Garnering his Pandoric courage, Malarkey takes down the box, removes his helmet and gloves, sits on a stepladder, and opens the box. He sifts through the papers before coming upon one in particular, a piece of Andrea's original artwork done in original crayon on Arches paper, hand-signed and dated by the artist in the lower right-hand corner:

F is for firm; A is for adorable; T is for terrific; H is for handsome; E is for exuberant; R is for reliable.

Malarkey thinks back a decade earlier to that particular day. You see, as Malarkey ages, the word "nostalgia" is more aligned with its original meaning of νόστος a "return home" rather than something merely sentimental. And so, Malarkey thinks back to that specific day and recalls a banner outside her Citrus City Montessori school that reads: HAPPY FATHER'S DAY. And he also sees Andrea running out of the school with her pink Sailor Moon backpack on, waving the artwork she's created. She rushes up to Malarkey who lifts her in his arms and kisses her as she shows him what she's done. He kisses her again and then as quickly as he was in the year 2010 Malarkey is back in his garage in 2022, sitting on a step ladder, trying with difficulty to control his emotions, as he gingerly replaces the artwork in the box, shelves it and nostalgically leaves the garage thinking to himself once again that after many a summer dies the swan.

CHAPTER EIGHTEEN

CETERIS PARIBUS & ALL THAT JAZZ

That night Malarkey, Andrea, and Liliana walk into the Citrus City Grille for dinner. The manager, Aristotle Aristopoulous, a balding, mid-fifties Greek, knows Professor Malarkey well, since Malarkey often comes there for dinner or for a glass of Lillet. Aristotle walks up to him beaming, arms outstretched.

"Professor Malarkey. Good to see you again," he says, hugging him and kissing him on both cheeks.

"Ari, this is my daughter, Andrea, and my friend, Liliana."

"My pleasure. Usual table?"

"Yes."

Andrea walks behind Aristotle as Malarkey and Liliana follow.

"Friend?" asks Liliana. "Is that what you called me? Your friend? Why not sleeping buddy or your vaginal vagabond?"

"Lil, what else am I going to say?"

"Say anything, but don't call me your *friend*."

"How's cuddly concubine?"

"What a wordsmith. I'm surprised the university pays you for that."

"I'm surprised the university pays me at all."

They all sit down.

"I'll send someone over right away," Aristotle says.

"So, where were we?" Malarkey asks.

"Well, Andrea and I were talking economics," Malarkey's cuddly concubine answers.

"Right. Economics. I remember a bit of that. Lemme think. Oh, right! *Ceteris paribus* and all that jazz."

The two women look at each other and immediately begin to laugh.

"Ceteris paribus!"

In case the Reader has no clue what *Ceteris paribus* is, Malarkey will define it according to Wikipedia: "One of the disciplines in which ceteris paribus clauses are most widely used is economics, in which they are employed to simplify the formulation and description of economic outcomes. When using ceteris paribus in economics, one assumes that all other variables except those under immediate consideration are held constant. For example, it can be predicted that if the price of beef increases—ceteris paribus—the quantity of beef demanded by buyers will decrease. In this example, the clause is used to operationally describe everything surrounding the relationship between both the price and the quantity demanded of an ordinary good." This definition is more than Malarkey remembers and that's why he's quoting it.

"What's so funny?"

"We don't really say that anymore," says Andrea.

"Worked for me when I was an undergraduate."

"Darling, when you were an undergraduate, Keynes was an undergraduate."

Both Liliana and Andrea find that raucously amusing. Malarkey, who feels totally out of it, turns to the Reader directly as if to plead his case.

"Have you ever noticed that old age jokes seem a lot funnier when you're not?"

Malarkey isn't going to go into detail about what they order for dinner or what they talk about during or after dinner since it's all inconsequential. Malarkey will, however, talk about an incident later that evening that could very well continue the "after many a summer, dies the swan" leitmotif, but he won't. Suffice to say that back home, Malarkey is reading Beckett's *Waiting for Godot*. It's not the first time he reads Godot. As a matter of fact, Malarkey has read *Godot* so many times it's his license plate number: GODOT82. There are a couple Guinness Bitters on the coffee table. Andrea, who is sitting across from Malarkey, vapes and reads something by Stiglitz.

"What's that smell? Patchouli?" Malarkey asks, putting down *Godot*.

"Cinnamon buns," Andrea answers.

"Right. Cinnamon buns. Is that a scent or the title of a porno site?"

Andrea ignores him.

"Listen, I gotta ask you a serious question," Malarkey says.

"Oooo. Serious. Which is?"

Malarkey hesitates.

"Liliana and I have been talking about, well, kids."

"Eating them or having them?" Andrea answers in between puffs of cinnamon buns.

"Where'd you get that gene?"

"Apple from the tree and all that jazz. What's your question?"

"What would you think if, someday, the two of us got pregnant?"

Andrea blows a smoke ring.

"That's incest and it's a disgusting idea. I could report you for that."

"C'mon."

"My immediate response?"

"No, your delayed response."

Ignoring him as she often does, Andrea blows another smoke ring.

"My immediate response is to ask you if you have the energy."

"For what?"

"I mean, you've probably forgotten all about what it takes to raise a kid."

"Not everything."

"No, just the part where toddlers shit themselves and then wipe it on the walls."

"Did you do that?"

"No, you did."

"Oh, right. TMI."

"Listen, dad, I think Liliana is terrific and I know she wants kids, but I don't have to tell you that's something that will change your life even beyond your imagination and that's scary enough."

"What's that mean?"

"Means I gave one of your novels to a roommate and she asked if you had written that before or after you were institutionalized."

"Funny, but you're equivocating."

"Okay, let me leave it at this. I couldn't have asked for a better, more loving father. You have always been there for me whenever I've needed you for whatever reason I've needed you and whatever you choose to do I will always support and love you."

Andrea inhales.

"So, you're not going to answer the question?"

Andrea exhales.

"I just did. But as long as we're having this father-daughter bonding moment."

"Yes?"

"I'm thinking of taking a trip to Europe this summer."

Malarkey pauses. Does not see that coming. Goes back to Estragon.

"Well, as long as you're *thinking* about it, then *think* all you want. Actually, you might want to *ponder* that idea, which is thinking on steroids."

"No, it's more than thinking about it at this point. A couple of my friends and I are planning it."

"I see. Not sure I think that's a good idea. I recommend pondering."

"Why not?"

Malarkey puts down Vladimir.

"You know, young girls traveling alone, foreign countries, foreign men." He wiggles his fingers as if he were trying to scare her. "That sort of thing. Scary, very scary. Not to mention terrorism, the potential crash of the global economy and new Covid viruses. I mean you don't want to be stranded in someplace like the Uffizi during an economic downturn, do you?"

Malarkey returns to Pozzo.

"Uh, huh."

"Maybe when you're older. More mature. Able to lift your own luggage."

"I'll be twenty-one in June."

"My, my, my. How quickly time passes. Well, in the unlikely event this would happen, how would you plan to pay for this Siddarthian journey?"

"I've been saving for it."

"Since when?"

"Since I was a freshman."

"Impressive."

"Maybe you should wait until your senior year and then you'll have all you need."

"Like Godot?"

"Huh?"

"Dad, I'm not asking for permission. I'm just sharing my plans with you."

Malarkey puts down Pozzo and Lucky and nods as if to confirm to himself that Andrea is no longer a child. It's one of those "ah-hah moments" in a parent's life. Clearly, a "swan moment" in a parent's life when the reality of the where-one-is-in-life clashes with the reality of where-one-has-been-in-life. But even Malarkey knows that. To those Readers who haven't had children this may seem like a foreign concept. The actual confrontation between the past that has manifested as the present and the present that will persist into the future as a reminder that children grow up, parents age, and death is not a theory.

At that point, that realization upon him, Malarkey stands up, walks over to Andrea, and kisses her on the forehead.

"I love you," he says, without dialogue tags.

Then he turns and walks toward his bedroom as Andrea looks on.

"Papi."

He turns.

"I love you, too."

Malarkey nods as a way of reconfirming the obvious and walks off. Malarkey isn't going to talk about what happens to him in his bedroom though he mumbles some verse by Yeats. If the Reader can't figure that out then, perhaps, the Reader hasn't had children or, perhaps, the Reader has had children, but denies the fact they grow up and they need them less. If the former, then you should be crying; if the latter, then it's just a matter of time before you will.

CHAPTER NINETEEN

RETURN TO LAX

Return to LAX. Malarkey, Liliana, and Andrea pull up in Liliana's Beemer. They get out of the car and remove Andrea's luggage from the trunk. At the same time, the cop from the arrival scene shows up and sees Malarkey and Liliana as Malarkey opens the passenger door for her. One might think the cop's return is serendipitous. If one thinks that, then one would be absolutely right.

"Busy man," the cop says, smiling one of his unforgettable police smiles.

"Sorry," Malarkey responds.

The cop looks at Liliana and nods.

"Let me guess. Your other daughter?"

"No, I'm his steady lay. I'll bet you'd like a piece of it, wouldn't you?"

The cop is gobsmacked by her response. Malarkey smiles at him, raises his eyebrows, gets in the car and the two of them drive off.

CHAPTER TWENTY

BACK AT CITRUS CITY COLLEGE

With Thanksgiving break concluded, the conflagration of returning to classes and the maelstrom of meetings begin again. One might think it's much ado about nothing given the tradeoff of having five months off per year. One could certainly make that argument. Certainly, Malarkey can make that argument, but beyond the maelstrom of meetings and the apoplexy of photocopying, there's also the surfeit of surprises. One such surprise occurs when Malarkey checks his mail in the English office. While standing next to the closed door of Rabinowitz's office Malarkey can't help but overhear a disconcerting conversation going on inside between Rabinowitz and one of his female colleagues, Julia, an assistant professor who has plans for promotion and tenure. Now, for some Readers, promotion and tenure might mean nothing and at some time in the future, after it disappears, it might mean nothing to a faculty member as well, but at this time, promotion and tenure mean that if Julia receives it then she and her husband are financially secure, can start a family and, possibly, rent a larger apartment (home buying in Citrus City and environs is out of the question on a faculty salary). In other words, she doesn't have to go back on the job market again and again and again *ad astra*. So, the Reader can imagine how frightening the following dialogue is to Julia.

"I can't keep it in any longer. I'm obsessed by you. I can't stop thinking about you. There I've said it," Rabinowitz blurts. "Day, night, even with my wife."

"Professor Rabinowitz, I don't know what to say. I'm a happily married woman. This is very uncomfortable for me especially since I'm going up for tenure and that's in your hands."

"Ah, hah, if you were in my hands, there'd be nothing to worry about. Please be in my hands, my arms, my . . ."

"I'm sorry, but, but I can't listen to this. I have to leave."

"No, please, Julia, don't go."

Distraught, Julia, a very attractive, thirtyish brunette, comes bolting out of the office as the pot-bellied Rabinowitz, balding with untidy wisps of wiry hair and tortoise shell glasses taped at the temples, neurotically chases after her, but abruptly stops after he sees Malarkey standing next to the door by the mailbox, fanning himself with his mail, at which point Rabinowitz points a finger at him.

"And you didn't hear anything!"

Malarkey raises his eyebrows.

"I heard everything I needed to hear and if you don't take that finger out of my face you'll find it shoved where the sun don't shine."

Rabinowitz rushes back inside his office and slams the door as Malarkey looks at the Reader.

"Now you might think that exercise in sexual harassment

would have been the end of the road for old Rabinowitz, but you'd be wrong. After Julia filed a sexual harassment claim, the administration eventually removed him as chair of the department and, because of Citrus City's early Christian roots, promoted him to Assistant Dean of Gender Equity and Ecumenical Flagellation, a promotion that actually garnered him more money, more prestige and more respect, at least from anyone who might be an advocate of sexual harassment. As for Julia, in spite of Rabinowitz's mediocre recommendation, she garners tenure and promotion based on her research and performance in the classroom. Life in the academy. As Vonnegut might say, "So it goes."

CHAPTER TWENTY-ONE

TUTORIAL TIME WITH PROFESSOR MALARKEY

The Reader needs to read this scene as if it were out of a film. Given the fact the Reader may not be used to reading such scenes, Malarkey will help you out.

EXT. MALARKEY'S OFFICE-DAY

Liliana knocks on Malarkey's door and he opens it. She's well-coiffed and made up to look as if she's going out on the town and stands with books in her arms. They speak very formally since there are several students sitting in the hallway.

LILIANA

Good morning, Professor Malarkey.

MALARKEY

(smiling)

Good morning, Miz Liliano. What can I do for you?

LILIANA
I'd like to discuss a few academic things with you if you have the time.

MALARKEY
Absolutely. Please come in.

LILIANA
Why thank you.

Liliana walks in and Malarkey closes the door. This time he locks it. Imagine the remainder of this scene in FAST FORWARD. If you want, you can listen to Beethoven again, but it's not mandatory. Liliana flings her books to the floor and the two of them rip off their clothes and have sex on his desk, on the floor, on the desk again, in the swivel chair, doggie style, missionary style, whatever ever style you can think of after which time they hastily re-dress, and she picks up her books and brushes her hair.

As Malarkey opens the door for Liliana, the scene returns to NORMAL despite both of them being clearly the worse for wear. Malarkey's shirt is untucked and his belt hangs limply in front of his zipper. Liliana tries to brush her hair, which is in flyaway mode. As she steps out of the office the other students in the hallway look at both of them rather strangely having heard what has just transpired in the office.

LILANA
Thank you, Professor Malarkey for pointing out my weaknesses.

MALARKEY
The pleasure has been all mine. Don't hesitate to come
again.

Liliana leaves, slightly turning her ankle as she walks down
the hall while Malarkey smiles sheepishly at the students
waiting in the hallway then closes the door.

Should this novel be made into a film, don't expect to see
this scene. Much too bawdy even for Malarkey.

FADE OUT TO NEXT CHAPTER

CHAPTER TWENTY-TWO

THE FINGER OF LITTLE MISUNDERSTANDING

It just so happens that later the same day Malarkey has an appointment with his urologist. It's not his first appointment nor is it going to be his last. It's a follow-up appointment as it's called. The assistant escorts him to an examining room and hands him a gown, which Malarkey puts on with little fanfare and sits on the edge of the examining table as he scans a copy of *Wine & Food* magazine the cover of which has a picture of giblets made to look appetizing and in large black letters above the photo it reads: *GIBLETS FOR GOURMETS.*

At that moment, his urologist, Dr. Bako, walks in. Bako is in his early fifties, of medium height, slightly graying at the temples and wears very fashionable Prada glasses. Bako is strictly business, and has a very dry sense of humor that only a urologist might have. Or maybe a proctologist. He shakes Malarkey's hand, leans against a counter and folds his arms.

"Doctor Malarkey. How are you?"

"Fine, until I come here."

"Oh? And why is that?"

"Because sooner or later you're going to get personal."

"Absolutely, so let's do it sooner."

Bako turns around, grabs a pair of latex gloves, puts them on, slaps his hands together and squirts some KY onto the fingertips. It's the sound of a squirting tube that prequels the subsequent events.

"Did you know your name in Hungarian means axe man?" Malarkey asks, trying to postpone the inevitable.

"Yes, I did and that's why I became a urologist. You remember the pose?"

Malarkey rolls his eyes, sighs and climbs onto the examining table, bending over with his chest as far as possible to his thighs so that his ass faces the Reader. Bako raises the gown and at that moment, he sticks his finger up Malarkey's ass. The Reader needs to try to imagine Malarkey's face as it contorts. There's no photo Malarkey can possibly use to illustrate this discomfort. So, the grimace on Malarkey's face has to be manufactured by you the Reader. If you're a male over fifty, then it probably isn't much of a stretch for you to imagine the grimace on Malarkey's face yourself. If you're a female, then Malarkey has no analogy for that. Malarkey imagines that, perhaps, a Pap smear might be analogous, but since he's never had a Pap smear he doesn't know for sure. Actually, a Pap smear sounds worse.

Minutes later, a fully dressed Malarkey sits in Bako's office. Medical degrees and fellowships hang on the wall, medical books line the bookshelves, photos of family abound. Bako is at his computer typing away as Malarkey sits somewhat uncomfortably across from him, slightly squirming from the after-effects of the rectal exam. Bako quits typing and turns to face a fidgeting Malarkey across his desk.

"So, how's your social life?"

"You mean, like dating?"

"Yes, like dating. From what I gather that's what you're doing."

"Well, yes, I'm dating."

"Really? So, how's that going?"

"Hmm. She's a wee bit younger."

"How much younger is a wee bit?"

"She's thirty-six."

Bako raises his eyebrows.

"That could cause some stress. Does she have kids?"

"No."

"Have you talked about that?"

"She has. Kinda."

"Kinda yes or kinda no? It's not a trick question, professor."

"I'm of two minds."

"I imagine she's of one. What's the problem? Too much sex or lack of it?"

Malarkey raises his eyebrows as Bako returns to the computer, reads something then turns back to Malarkey and crosses his arms across his chest.

"You need a higher dose of sildenafil?"

Malarkey shakes his head.

"Not yet."

"If you need more let me know."

"Top of my list, doc."

Bako shifts into a more serious mode.

"Couple of things, professor. You emailed me to place an order for a semen analysis, but you haven't done it. Is that part of the dating process?"

"Yes, well, no."

"Why not?"

"Not sure I want to know."

"Know what?"

"Whether my fellas can swim or not."

"But I imagine she wants to know."

Malarkey nods.

"So, when will you do it?"

"Sooner or later."

"What's the issue?"

"Something odd about jerking off in a cup."

"Pretend you're in college and it's a sock. You'll be fine."

Bako smiles and turns back to the computer.

"Over the past year your PSA has varied from five-point-one to five-point-eight. Just a reminder. If you're going to take a PSA test don't have sex for several days before."

"Because?"

"Because it skews the results."

"Up or down?"

"Up, but I don't find your results that alarming."

"Is there something you do find alarming?"

"Yes, well, not necessarily alarming, but I'm disinclined to take another biopsy since we've done two and I'm not a big fan of them."

"Because?"

"Because there's risk involved. After the last biopsy, there were only trace amounts of cancer. We talked about that and that's why you're on active surveillance."

Malarkey looks somewhat preoccupied.

"Something bothering you, professor?"

"To be honest, it's a bit disconcerting to wake up every morning knowing cancer cells are dancing in my prostate and the phrase 'active surveillance' seems like something a Navy Seal might do."

"Well, there's always the option of not waking up at all, isn't there?" Bako answers with a smile. "Let me reassure you about something."

"What's that?"

Bako leans back in his chair and crosses his arms across his chest.

"That you'll probably die *with* it rather than *from* it, though there's no guarantee. See me in six months."

Malarkey is not at all reassured.

"Could I ask you a question?"

"Ask away."

"Are courses in bedside manner an elective in medical school?"

Bako smiles.

"They certainly are, they certainly are."

CHAPTER TWENTY-THREE

GET DOWN TONIGHT

After the digital exercise is over for another six months, Malarkey carefully climbs into his XKE and drives out of the lot. As Malarkey cruises up the 405N, he turns on the radio and hears K.C. & The Sunshine Band singing, "Get Down Tonight." Now if the Reader doesn't know the lyrics or has forgotten them, here's a sample:

> Baby, baby, let's get together
> Honey, honey, me and you
> And do the things, ah, do the things
> That we like to do

Of course, without the music this chapter tends to lose its impact. So, as with previous chapters, Malarkey suggests the Reader Google the song and play it while reading the chapter as Malarkey does the same while writing it. Malarkey has helped you out here (https://www.youtube.com/watch?v=31FpTAD7smE). You can begin now.

Now by the time Malarkey gets to campus, it's midday

and even though K.C. is still ringing in his ears, he realizes the necessity of grading some papers, presumably those more recent than 1988.

> Oh, do a little dance, make a little love
> Get down tonight, get down tonight
> Do a little dance, make a little love
> Get down tonight, get down tonight

So, Malarkey attempts to grade papers while sitting on his favorite campus bench, but it becomes increasingly difficult to do so since, even though sorority rush is over, there are bevvies of young co-eds wearing very, very short cutoff jeans or very, very short shorts that pass by and there are rapid cuts from Malarkey's point of view to those nubile young women whose butt cheeks *à la mode* are mostly hanging outside their shorts rather than inside them and which tend to bounce in unison to K.C.'s music.

> Baby, baby, I'll meet you
> Same place, same time
> Where we can get together
> And ease up our mind

Perhaps, if Malarkey were younger this would be a fanciful distraction in the same way fanciful distractions go, but Malarkey has just come from his urologist who has confirmed, in no uncertain terms, that his prostate cancer will not go on hiatus and, as a bonus, has given him a higher dosage of sildenafil for his erectile dysfunction.

Oh, do a little dance, make a little love
Get down tonight, whoo, get down tonight, hey
Do a little dance, make a little love
Get down tonight, get down tonight, baby

These are symptoms that someone from the Woodstock Nation would never have imagined while smoking weed and fucking in between sets of Richie Havens and Country Joe or Joe Cocker and Jimi Hendrix. So it goes.

Get down, get down, get down, get down, get down tonight baby
Get down, get down, get down, get down, get down tonight baby
Get down, get down, get down, get down, get down tonight baby
Get down, get down, get down, get down, get down tonight baby
Get down, get down, get down, get down, get down tonight baby
Get down, get down, get down, get down, get down tonight baby

CHAPTER TWENTY-FOUR

PROFESSOR WINDOW DRESSING AND ALL THAT JAZZ

Malarkey gives up grading papers. There are only so many bare butts one prof can deal with at one time and he heads to the English department where he's been summoned by Herr Rabinowitz who, as Malarkey enters the office, sits behind a very misogynistically messy desk. Malarkey's desk is also messy, but at least it's controlled messiness and not misogynistic. The difference between the two is simple: Controlled Messiness is evinced by an organization in which the Controller knows absolutely where things are regardless of the apparent messiness; Uncontrolled Messiness is akin to slovenliness, which, in Rabinowitz's case, is equal to his measure.

"So, why have you summoned me here, mi'lord?" Malarkey asks, arms crossed in front of him as a way of protecting himself against anything bacterial that might be hiding in the stacks of messiness on Rabinowitz's desk or that might spring to life from anything he may have touched.

"You need to take over Professor Poshlust's grad creative writing class for two weeks."

Before Malarkey gets into the reasons why he has to do this, the Reader needs to know a little bit about Poshlust who was recruited by a former Dean whom the latter met when he was Dean of Humanities at Quincunx College outside Portland, Oregon. When Poshlust arrived at Citrus City College, he came assuming he was a household name even though most of the faculty never heard of him. It wasn't as if John Barth or Kurt Vonnegut or Philip Roth or Robert Coover or Malcolm Bradbury or John Fowles were dropped on our doorstep and over time, the English faculty was forced to listen to his two favorite lines which were, "I'm not just window dressing" and "When I went to Iowa," the latter phrase being a shibboleth for all of us to know that decades ago he attended an MFA program that allegedly put all those who graduated from such a program immediately into the Pantheon of Great American Writers. Of course, that would exclude such American writers as Pynchon and Markson, Heller and Berryman all of whom somehow managed to become great writers without ever attending Iowa. He also looked with enormous disdain on any writer who didn't write like he did. In other words, experimental writers were eschewed as merely playing "mind games." Of course, that suggestion was patently ludicrous since it included but was not limited to such "mind game" writers as: Abish, Arlt, Aragon, Beckett, Borges, Barth, Calvino, Coover, Cortázar, and just about every other writer living or dead whose last name fell in between the letters A and Z who realized that copying Balzac was not only unimaginative, but, well, facile-minded.

But Poshlust was always promoting himself and was especially adept at name-dropping even though many of the names he dropped were as unknown as his own. Even the president of his former college once opined that, "He was the master of short story writing." Whether the president ever read Poshlust is debatable and those who had read his writing weren't soon forgetting Chekhov, Poe, or Joyce, not to mention Borges, but he had fashioned an image that seemed to precede him wherever he went and the college lauded him with award upon award (not to mention salary increases upon salary increases) simply because no one ever really took the time to read his work. Of course, when Poshlust exclaimed in a faculty meeting that he thought Stephen King was as "good as Faulkner," Malarkey knew the entire department was fucked.

"You mean, Professor I'm-not-window-dressing, ass-kissing? That Professor Poshlust?"

"What?"

"Never mind. Why me? There are plenty of other lackeys here who can teach that course."

"Yes, but you're at the top of the lackey list. Anyway, he's been invited to teach at Stanford for two weeks and I need you to take over his class."

"Oooo. Stanford. Is he now sucking off the tit of the Stanford Cardinal even though cardinals have no tits? Seems he's always being invited somewhere. How's he do that, mi'lord?"

"Because he's an accomplished writer."

"And me?"

"You're not."

"How sad? How very, very sad. So, when do I get this plum teaching assignment?"

Rabinowitz looks at his watch.

"Two hours."

"Brilliant. Plenty of prep time."

"Prep time, schmep time. Do whatever you want. I'm busy."

Rabinowitz waves him off and as Malarkey leaves, he winks at the Reader who should know that something Malarkian is in store.

Now while all this is going on, the Reader finds Liliana sitting on a park bench at nearby Hart Park reading a copy of *Virginia Woolf's Shorter Fiction*; however, her attention is soon drawn from *Kew Gardens* to several young mothers who are playing with their children: on the slide, on a swing, on a merry-go-round, in a sandbox. She ponders that sight, those sights, for several moments, looks at her watch, closes her book and leaves the park. The Reader can speculate on what Liliana is pondering. In the unlikely event the Reader has no clue as to what she's pondering it will manifest in due time.

It just so happens (as is often the case in fiction) the class Liliana is on her way to attend is the same class Malarkey is going to teach and as Malarkey enters the classroom, the dozen or so students, including Liliana, are sitting in a circle chatting about whatever. (It's not important to the storyline.) Malarkey walks in with his computer tucked under his arm, immediately sees Liliana and they acknowledge each other with complementary raised eyebrows. Make of that what you will. Pretend they're close-ups and they're re-enacting the eating scene out of *Tom Jones*, but without the food. As Malarkey downloads a YouTube site, he addresses the class:

"I'm not introducing myself since, as I've been told, my reputation precedes me." He looks at Liliana who looks back and smiles.

"For the next two weeks, I'm subbing for Mister Poshlust while he pretends to be an important American writer who's been invited to Stanford. As all of you are starving writers or eventually will be I'd like to play what should be or become your national anthem."

Malarkey flips off the lights and clicks on the YouTube site and the Reader hears the Bee Gees sing the four-minute version of "Stayin' Alive." Malarkey doesn't really need to restate what he's restated, but if he has to restate it the Reader should watch the same excerpt on YouTube while s/he reads the rest of this chapter: (https://www.youtube.com/watch?v=I_izvAbhExY).

As the students (and the Reader) watch and listen to clips of *Saturday Night Fever*, Malarkey starts dancing from the front of the classroom toward the back. At first, the class looks on somewhat astonished by his behavior, but, soon, one at a time, the students get up and start dancing as Malarkey "boogies" his way toward Liliana and the two of them dance as intimately as two can dance in a classroom without violating Citrus City College's rules of faculty classroom behavior.. Malarkey attempts, as best as he can, to imitate John Travolta; however, imitating Travolta at his age has enormous medical repercussions, but he does his best.

After a short time, he and Liliana turn and "bump" bums at which point the music and the classroom scene fade out and Malarkey and Liliana are now seen lying nude in her bed. A Voluspa *Tuberosa di Notte* burns. Incense wafts through the room. The Bee Gees play "How Deep Is Your Love." No pun intended. Malarkey looks lovingly at Liliana, but is clearly out of breath; she, not so much, and the Reader has to read his breathlessness in his dialogue.

"Did you?"

"I did."

"Was it?"

"Yes, it was."

"Did I?"

"Yes, you did."

"You know, I could get sacked for this."

"For what?"

"This."

"But I said I did."

"I know."

"So, don't worry about getting sacked."

"I'm not sure we're on the same page here."

"No, we're not."

She rolls on top of him and they kiss.

End of chapter.

CHAPTER TWENTY-FIVE

HAIL TO THEE, US NEWS & WORLD REPORT

Every year, USNWR comes out with a ranking of the best colleges in the United States. The most current edition of "Best Colleges" is ostensibly established "to help domestic and international students compare the academic quality of US-based schools that includes data on nearly 1,800 colleges and features rankings of 1,376 schools" and for thirty plus years, they pride themselves as being the only organization that has been ranking colleges. Some universities and colleges are always at or near the top: Princeton, Harvard, Yale, Williams, Amherst, Carleton. But there are also regional rankings as well and every year Citrus City College looks forward to where it ranks. Coming from Oxford, Malarkey thinks these rankings are at least arbitrary and at most a waste of his time. So, it's with some astonishment to other faculty members that Malarkey walks out of his office wearing his scarlet and gray Oxford gown as a number of other professors—each of whom wears their own doctoral gowns—gather to proceed to the campus center for the yearly tribute to the USNWR rankings. A professor of divinity, whose office is next to Malarkey's walks up to him with a puzzled look on his face.

"I didn't think you attended these things," he says.

"Missed last year. Hope it didn't bring down our rankings."

"So, why go this year? You want to be noticed?"

"Maybe, but I just want to be part of the tradition," he humbly says, raising his eyebrows.

Like monks on a pilgrimage, the professors move solemnly from their respective offices and head outside where, hanging from the roof of one of the buildings, an enormous thirty-foot banner reads in bold letters:

US NEWS AND WORLD REPORT DAY
CITRUS CITY COLLEGE
#2 REGIONAL UNIVERSITIES WEST BY SOUTHWEST

In the plaza, outside Phigmente Hall, about one hundred black-robed professors stand with heads bent, hands clasped to their chests. Each year, the entourage is led by a different Dean, and on this particular day it is led by the Dean of the School of Phlegmatic Sciences who, standing alone on a dais, raises both his arms to the sky and recites, "In the name of *US News and World Report*, we beseech you to shed grace upon our humble institution. You may all now strike the pose," at which point all the professors kneel and genuflect toward the sign and as they do, looking like something out of Eco's *Name of the Rose*, they chant in unison, "Usnew, We Are Thankful, Usnew, We Are Thankful!" repeatedly. Malarkey, who's tucked in the middle of that huddled mass of black robes, yet identifiable by his scarlet and gray gown, suddenly stands up and, amid that black mass, starts running around as if his hair is on fire.

"We're number two! We're number two! We're number two! We're number two! Bless you, Usnew! Bless you." Malarkey continues to scream as he rushes around the mass of genuflecting professors eventually ending up in the Chancellor's office later the same day. The Chancellor is not happy. It's as if he's reached his proverbial tether with Malarkey's behavior.

"Why'd you do that, Malcolm?"

"Because these rankings are ludicrous. Why are we gen-uflecting to a bloody magazine?"

"It's a tradition."

"So is circumcision, but not every guy gets his dick clipped."

Jones is not at all amused.

"Malcolm, by the end of the school year you should seri-ously think about taking that sabbatical," he says with a furrowed brow.

"But I don't want to take a sabbatical," Malarkey answers with a furrowed brow.

"Didn't you say you were leaving for Carmel this weekend?"

"Yes. My birthday."

Jones raises his eyebrows.

"Then while you're there celebrating your birthday think about it, Malcolm. Will you think about it?"

Malarkey nods, but more out of deference than interest since he knows even if he takes a sabbatical it's going to cost him some cash he doesn't have not to mention the fact his manifold meetings with the Chancellor would be dramatically reduced.

"Won't you miss these meetings, Chancellor?" Malarkey asks.

"Trust me," was his answer. "Think about it."

CHAPTER TWENTY-SIX

CASANOVA'S RESTAURANT; OR A NIGHT TO BE REMEMBERED

The trip to Carmel has been planned for quite some time and though they have only been a couple for a few months, Malarkey is more than willing to let Liliana handle all the arrangements and that's why they end up staying at L'Auberge Hotel rather than the Econo Lodge in Salinas. This is L'Auberge Hotel:

This is the Econo Lodge in Salinas:

You get the picture. For some Readers, the fact Liliana and Malarkey have become a couple so quickly may seem "unrealistic." For those Readers, you need to understand that even though the romance begins *at* college it isn't a college romance. Nor is it a Hugh Grant-Andie McDowell romance. To remind Readers who, for one reason or another, may have forgotten, Malarkey will remind you: Liliana is a widow; Malarkey is a divorced father of a college-age woman. Their relationship has transcended the sophomoric stage of relationships as their private advising sessions can attest. And with that, you can return to the reading.

Liliana has not been to Carmel, but Malarkey has talked about it quite a bit and one of his favorite restaurants there is Casanova's. Now, as their website states, Casanova's has a unique history, which Malarkey here shares: "In 1977, Aunt Fairy Bird's house, which had fallen into disrepair, was remodeled. The design was a blend of our family's old farmhouse in Belgium, with elements of the warmth and richness of our childhood memories, and the character of the old house itself. Great attention was given to every detail to maintain the spirit of the old residence. We kept the original floor plan and added the outdoor fountain patio. In 1987, we excavated fourteen feet under the restaurant to build a cellar for our world-class wine selection. In 1997, Casanova expanded by purchasing the adjacent property and adding two more dining rooms, a large second kitchen and a small, covered garden patio. In 2003, we built a room to house 'Van Gogh's Table,' the table at which Vincent Van Gogh ate his daily meals while boarding at the Auberge Ravoux in Auvers Sur-Oise, France. Casanova is constantly evolving and inspiring those that visit us. The 'Casanova style' has become well known to numerous designers and architects and it has echoed throughout numerous homes and commercial buildings in Carmel and beyond." It's one of the most romantic restaurants in all of Carmel. Period.

At that time of the year, the restaurant is festively festooned with Christmas lights and other holiday paraphernalia. The style, décor, food reflect the small inns of France and Italy, but words clearly can't do it justice so here's a picture of the outside:

And here's the table at which Malarkey and Liliana sit:

Very romantic. Now the Reader has to imagine even though the table is empty they will sit across from each other beneath the tree. At that moment, however, she looks at Malarkey who, from her point of view, is talking with the *maître d'* in a rather suspicious manner, looking over his shoulder at Liliana as if she's going to sneak up on him, then back to the *maître d'* before escorting him into the kitchen where they both seemingly disappear. Moments later Malarkey walks out of the kitchen and returns to their table. Malarkey is so transparent.

"What's the secret?" she asks.

"What secret?"

"Oh, Malcolm, sometimes you're so predictable."

"It's one of the virtues of being an asshole."

At that moment, the waiter, Jean-Paul, mid-twenties and very French walks up to them.

"Bon soir. I am Jean-Paul. I will be your waiter tonight."
He looks at Liliana. "Would you like to start with an apéritif?"

"I'll have a page out of *Nausea*," Malarkey says, an allusion to Sartre, which no one in the restaurant but Malarkey gets.

"Monsieur?"

Realizing most everyone in the restaurant, including Liliana, is gazing at him strangely, he decides not to pursue any allusion to Existentialism and turns instead to the menu.

"Uh, yes, would you like a glass of Lillet," he says to Liliana.

She nods.

"Lillet Blanc or Rouge?" Jean-Paul asks.

"Blanc," she answers.

"Two Blanks," Malarkey says to a wincing Jean-Paul who leaves puzzled as to why of all the tables in the restaurant he gets stuck with Malarkey's.

"Why do you do that?"

"Do what?"

"Say something patently ridiculous like two blanks."

"Sometimes trying to be clever is a burden."

"Then try to stifle yourself. Now let's talk about us."

And they do. They talk about their relationship. Some very intimate things that the Reader isn't really privy to so Malarkey will not divulge them. In due course, some of those things will be revealed, but not necessarily in a Dickensian manner. The Reader will have to wait patiently for that time. In the meantime, they look over the menu and after Jean-Paul brings two Lillets, they order.

"She'll have the duck?"

"I can order for myself. I'll have the duck."

"And for you, monsieur?"

"He'll have the beef."

"Yeah, the beef," he answers rather sheepishly.

"And to drink?"

"A bottle of the Brunello di Montalcino."

Liliana raises her eyebrows.

"Did you get a pay raise?"

"No raise yet, but I'm hoping to get lucky tonight."

Liliana shakes her head as if one more pun will ruin dinner. Malarkey winks at the waiter who embarrassingly smiles and walks away. Not long after they've ordered, Jean-Paul brings the plates and sets them on the table, then opens the bottle of wine and offers Malarkey a taste.

"It'll do."

Jean-Paul raises his eyebrows, but pours glasses for both and they begin to toast.

"You do know that red wine with duck is not *de rigueur*, right?" Liliana asks.

"It's *de rigueur* if I'm paying for it."

They clink glasses.

"To us," he says.

"What a wordsmith."

As Malarkey has written, if this were a Dickensian novel, then Malarkey would tell you all sorts of things about what they talk about at dinner, but it's not a Dickensian novel so there's no need for that. Actually, at this point, it reads more like a Fielding novel and what ensues at dinner is clearly Fieldingesque. As Jean-Paul brings the entrées to the table, a very strange thing begins to happen. Needing a rest from writing, Malarkey yields to Fielding who takes over from here.

"Heroes, notwithstanding the high ideas, which, by the

means of flatterers, they may entertain of themselves, or the world may conceive of them, have certainly more of mortal than divine about them. However elevated their minds may be, their bodies at least (which is much the major part of most) are liable to the worst infirmities, and subject to the vilest offices of human nature. Among these latter, the act of eating, which hath by several wise men been considered as extremely mean and derogatory from the philosophic dignity, must be in some measure performed by the greatest prince, hero, or philosopher upon earth; nay, sometimes Nature hath been so frolicsome as to exact of these dignified characters a much more exorbitant share of this office than she hath obliged those of the lowest order to perform.

When the Reader hath duly reflected on these many charms which all centered in Mr. Malarkey and considers at the same time the fresh obligations which Liliana has to him, it will be a mark more of prudery than candor to entertain a bad opinion of her because she conceived a very good opinion of him.

But, whatever censures may be passed upon her, it is my business to relate matters of fact with veracity. Liliana has, in truth, not only a good opinion of Mr. Malarkey, but a very great affection for him. That is, she is in love with him. To speak out boldly at once, she is in love, according to the present universally received sense of that phrase, by which love is applied indiscriminately to the desirable objects of all our passions, appetites, and senses, and is understood to be that preference which we give to one kind of food rather than to another.

But though the love to these several objects may possibly be one and the same in all cases, its operations however

must be allowed to be different; for, how much so ever we
may be in love with an excellent filet of beef or duck, or
bottle of Brunello di Montalcino; yet do we never smile,
nor ogle, nor dress, nor flatter, nor endeavor by any other
arts or tricks to gain the affection of the said beef, &c. Sigh
indeed we sometimes may; but it is generally in the absence,
not in the presence, of the beloved object. For otherwise we
might possibly complain of their ingratitude and deafness,
with the same reason as Pasiphae doth of her bull, whom
she endeavored to engage by all the coquetry practiced with
good success in the drawing-room on the much more sen-
sible as well as tender hearts of the fine gentlemen there.

The contrary happens in that love which operates between
persons of the same species, but not necessarily of different
sexes. Here we are no sooner in love than it becomes our
principal care to engage the affection of the object beloved.
For what other purpose indeed are our youth instructed in all
the arts of rendering themselves agreeable? If it was not with
a view to this love, I question whether any of those trades,
which deal in setting off and adorning the human person
would procure a livelihood. Nay, those great polishers of our
manners, who are by some thought to teach what principally
distinguishes us from the brute creation, even dancing-mas-
ters themselves, might possibly find no place in society. In
short, all the graces which young ladies—and young gentlemen to—learn from others, and the many improvements
which, by the help of a looking-glass, they add of their own,
are in reality those very *spicula et faces amoris* so often
mentioned by Ovid; or, as they are sometimes called in our
own language, the whole artillery of love.

Now Liliana and Malarkey had no sooner sat down

together than the former began to play this artillery upon the latter. But here, as we are about to attempt a description hitherto unassayed either in prose or verse, we think proper to invoke the assistance of certain aërial beings, who will, we doubt not, come kindly to our aid on this occasion.

"Say then, ye Graces! you that inhabit the heavenly mansions of Seraphina's countenance; for you are truly divine, are always in her presence, and well know all the arts of charming; say, what were the weapons now used to captivate the heart of Mr. Malarkey."

"First, from two lovely blue eyes, whose bright orbs flashed lightning at their discharge, flew forth two pointed ogles; but, happily for our hero, hit only a vast piece of beef which he was then conveying into his plate, and harmless spent their force. The fair warrior perceived their miscarriage, and immediately from her fair bosom drew forth a deadly sigh. A sigh, which none could have heard unmoved, and which was sufficient at once to have swept off a dozen beaus; so soft, so sweet, so tender, that the insinuating air must have found its subtle way to the heart of our hero, had it not luckily been driven from his ears by the coarse bubbling of some bottled water, which at that time he was pouring forth. Many other weapons did she assay; but the god of eating (if there be any such deity, for I do not confidently assert it) preserved his votary; or perhaps it may not be *dignus vindice nodus*, and the present security of Mr. Malarkey may be accounted for by natural means; for as love frequently preserves from the attacks of hunger, so may hunger possibly, in some cases, defend us against love.

"The fair one, enraged at her frequent disappointments, determined on a short cessation of arms. Which interval she employed in making ready every engine of amorous warfare for the renewing of the attack when dinner should be over.

"No sooner then was the cloth removed than she again began her operations. First, having planted her right eye sidewise against Mr. Malarkey, she shot from its corner a most penetrating glance; which, though great part of its force was spent before it reached our hero, did not vent itself absolutely without effect. This the fair one perceiving, hastily withdrew her eyes, and levelled them downward, as if she was concerned for what she had done; though by this means she designed only to draw him from his guard, and indeed to open his eyes, through which she intended to surprise his heart. And now, gently lifting up those two bright orbs, which had already begun to make an impression on poor Jones, she discharged a volley of small charms at once from her whole countenance in a smile. Not a smile of mirth, nor of joy; but a smile of affection, which most ladies have always ready at their command, and which serves them to show at once their good-humor, their pretty dimples, and their white teeth.

"This smile Mr. Malarkey receives full in his eyes, and is immediately staggered with its force. He then begins to see the designs of the enemy, and indeed to feel their success. A parley now was set on foot between the parties; during which the artful fair so slyly and imperceptibly carried on her attack, that she had almost subdued the heart of our hero before she again repaired to acts of hostility. In short, no sooner had the amorous parley ended and the lady had unmasked the royal battery, by carelessly letting her hand-kerchief drop from her neck, than the heart of Mr. Malarkey is entirely taken, and the fair conqueror enjoys the usual fruits of her victory."

Here the Graces think proper to end their description, and here we think proper to end the dining portion of the chapter and move on to dessert. Suffice to say, that after a marvelous dinner Jean-Paul returns to clear the plates and the stage is set for the amorous affair to follow.[6]

"And for dessert?"

Malarkey looks over the menu.

"What do you know! Apple Charlotte. You know my mother's name was Charlotte."

"I thought your mother's name was Molly."

"Molly, Charlotte what's the difference. They both have two syllables. We'll have two Charlottes."

Jean-Paul leaves.

"What if I don't want Apple Charlotte?"

"Then you'd be dishonoring my mother. You don't want to dishonor my mother, do you?"

"Sometimes you're incorrigible."

"Yes, and isn't that redeeming."

Momentarily, Jean-Paul returns with the desserts.

"Bon appétit."

They begin to eat, but Malarkey is more interested in noticing Liliana's reaction to tasting her dessert than to eating his. She puts a fork in it, but feels something hard. She stops.

"Anything wrong?"

"I'm not sure they prepared this very well."

"Why not?"

"There's something hard in here."

"Take it out. We'll order another. I'm not paying for a

---

[6] The Reader could, at this point, recall the food scene between Tom and Mrs. Waters, but much more sanguine. If the Reader doesn't know who these characters are, Malarkey feels for you.

poorly made Apple Charlotte!"

Malarkey starts to flag Jean-Paul when Liliana pulls out a small piece of parchment paper and begins to unwrap it revealing an antique white-gold engagement ring studded with tiny diamonds. Liliana is startled by the discovery and stares at Malarkey.

"Are you kidding me?"

"If it's half-baked we can send it back! No half-baked Apple Charlotte tonight! Garçon!"

She looks at the ring again.

"No, it's fully baked."

Realizing what the ring means, Liliana sheds a tear, then leans over the table and kisses Malarkey.

"Should we send it back?"

Liliana can only shake her head in reaction to yet another Malarkian malfeasance of emotion. Since the foreplay was more than aptly described by Mr. Fielding, there's no need to discuss what happens through the rest of dessert and the digestif and Malarkey can't describe it any better so let's return to L'Auberge where Malarkey and Liliana lie naked in bed.

A candle burns. Incense wafts. A Carmel moon casts blue-black light on the Egyptian cotton bedsheets, filling the room with a cascading glow that only accents the love they feel for one another. It's apparent by the heavy breathing; we have arrived at the *dénouement* or *la petite mort* of things depending on your take.

"Did you?"

"Kinda, yes."

"Was it?"

"Sort of."

"Did I?"

"I think so."

"You know, I could get sacked for this."

"For what?"

"This."

"But I said I did, kinda, yes."

"I know. Are we on the same page?"

"Not sure."

They kiss.

End of chapter.

As the Reader has discovered, many chapters end with "End of chapter." Even though it's axiomatic, Malarkey feels the need for closure to each chapter and closes that way. If the Reader doesn't appreciate this type of closure, then s/he is encouraged to substitute whatever closure s/he wishes. In large measure, it doesn't make a fucking difference to him. In this particular instance, one detects that even love cannot cure everything.

CHAPTER TWENTY-SEVEN

A FORMULA OF A DIFFERENT KIND

Formulas are great. There are formulas for everything. One can speak of a mathematical formula, a rule or principle expressed in algebraic symbols; or a medical prescription; or a detailed statement of ingredients such as in a recipe; or an expression of the constituents of a compound; or the specification of a racing car, which is often expressed in terms of engine capacity. Let's skip Archimedes' *Method of Exhaustion* since that's, well, exhausting and move on. In Malarkey's world, there's a formula for relationships, which he borrowed from Pythagoras and which he calls, *Malarkey's Theorem of Unrequited Angles*:

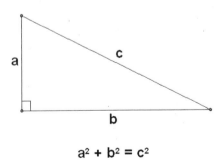

$$a^2 + b^2 = c^2$$

As the Reader must be aware, the Pythagorean Theorem is a trigonometric function defined as the sum of the areas of the two squares on the legs (a and b) equals the area of the square on the hypotenuse (c). For Malarkey, (a and b) equal the relative relationship between consenting adults which equals (c). In other words, the longer (a and b) are, for Malarkey, the better the chances of the relationship working out. If, in fact, the relationship does not work out for Malarkey, then he can always blame Pythagoras. This theorem has not worked out well for Malarkey, but he believes in mathematics and contends that it's the "mystery of the cosmos." Be that as it may, the formula Malarkey is dealing with now has nothing to do with relationships, but with race cars.

The morning after the night before, Liliana and Malarkey walk out of the hotel, but just as Malarkey starts to climb into the driver's side of the Jaguar, Liliana stops him.

"Not today."

"Not today, what?"

"I'm driving."

"Driving what?"

"You heard me. Get in."

So, Malarkey climbs into the passenger's seat as Liliana climbs behind the wheel.

"Look at me," she says.

"Is that an order or a request?"

"Just look at me."

Malarkey turns and Liliana takes out a kerchief and blindfolds him. The conversation continues with Malarkey blindfolded.

"Do I get a last request? This isn't one of those Al-Qaeda surprises, is it? I'd hate that surprise."

"Shut up. It's a birthday surprise."

"I'm not very keen on surprises. Last surprise I got was my ex suing me . . . again." The talk about exes isn't very appealing to Liliana because Malarkey has done that in the past. One thing Malarkey has a hard time learning (as do many divorced men) is that a current paramour does not necessarily want to hear about past relationships, let alone marriages. Not only is it somewhat disrespectful to said paramour, but it is self-defeating. Needless to say, the last thing Liliana wants to hear on Malarkey's birthday is anything having to do with the former Mrs. Malarkey.

"Can we make an agreement?"

"What's that?"

"Let's agree you won't talk about your ex anymore. Especially this weekend. The trip is for two, not three, and even an allusion to her won't fit in the car. Agreed?"

"Agreed," Malarkey replies, painfully embarrassed.

"I think you'll like this surprise."

They drive out of Carmel proper and take CA-68 East until they approach a sign that reads, LAGUNA SECA, 7 MILES, where Liliana turns into a restricted usage road. Another sign reads, SKIP BARBER RACING SCHOOL. Now if the Reader is a close Reader, then the Reader will recall in an earlier chapter there was a photograph of Malarkey with Jackie Stewart whom Malarkey once met through a good friend of his, the Brazilian Formula 1 racer Quincas Borba. How he met Stewart is irrelevant. Liliana pulls up and stops near the racetrack itself. She climbs out of the car, opens his door and leads him by the hand to the starting point of the racetrack.

"Are you ready?"

"Do I have a choice?"

When she removes the blindfold there's a fire engine red Formula One racecar awaiting him with Skip Barber standing next to it smiling and holding a racing helmet. Malarkey looks at the Reader and raises his eyebrows.

"Fuck!!!!!"

Malarkey has always had this fantasy of driving an F1 MacLaren and many times he has alluded to that during their brief, but intense, courtship. The fact Liliana remembers means a lot to Malarkey and the mere thought of driving Mazda Raceway at Laguna Seca is almost equal to taking an overdose of sildenafil. That's not to say he had an erection as he begins to drive the course only that it feels as if he has an erection.

To give the Reader an image of what Malarkey is soon to drive, he includes a map:

Alas, a MacLaren was not in offing. He really had no choice. His ride was a Renault R25 Formula 1, a baby F1, which, compared to a MacLaren, is the difference between a novel by Joyce and a short story by Chekhov. Both satisfying, but not the same. After he was instructed on what to do and not do, Malarkey settles into the driver's seat and adjusts his helmet, the harness and other accoutrements. Malarkey feels his heart rate increase, the palpitations in his pulse, the rapid breathing. There is no substitute for this kind of exhilaration and if the Reader has never climbed into one of these cars there is nothing Malarkey can write that would do justice to the experience.

Malarkey starts to drive the first of three laps around the course. He revs the engine. It gives him chills. And then, he starts. Slowly at first and then he eases into the gas and soon he's on his way. During the first lap he feels out the course. Down in one turn, up out of the turn, the cornering forces were something he has never anticipated, shifting onto a straightaway, shifting again, and again, the speed goes higher, he approaches another turn, braking, the smell of burning Dunlops, a down shift into the turn, and out and up and shifting again, his hands feel glued to the steering wheel, tighter than any steering wheel he's held, into another turn, and out, onto a straightaway shifting again, once, twice, three times, four times, at times he can't think fast enough, the car seems to have a mind of its own, by the time of his third and final lap, Malarkey feels as if he's one with car. At this point, the Reader has to imagine hearing the last three minutes of Beethoven's *Ninth*, *Ode to Joy*. To make it easy for you, click https://www.youtube.com/watch?v=B_5z0m7cs0A and listen to Lenny Bernstein as you imagine Malarkey taking each and every turn, dipping down, rising up, increasing speed, decreasing speed, downshifting. With each turn, the

Reader has to imagine cuts between Malarkey driving the final lap and his face, a face, though squashed in his helmet, showing unfettered enthusiasm. Even beneath the helmet, behind the plastic visor, one can see the thrill of driving, the joy of driving, of knowing that at any moment, at any second, life and death hang in the balance. A wrong move, an incorrect adjustment of the wheel, a thoughtless execution and it's all over. But that's not what Malarkey is thinking. His focus is on the track, on the handling of the car, on the music of Beethoven throbbing in his head. At the end of the circuit, as he crosses the finish line, as Malarkey finally stops the car and Beethoven ends, Malarkey removes his helmet and looks at the Reader. It's a bittersweet moment. The look is one of both joy and sadness.

"Fuck!!!!!!!!!!"

It is, after all, one less item on his bucket list. The wet spot on his pants is a testimony to that.

CHAPTER TWENTY-EIGHT

A FORMULA OF YET ANOTHER KIND

This formula is 1-[4-ethoxy-3-(6,7-dihydro-1-methyl-7-oxo-3-propyl-1H-pyrazolo[4,3-d]pyrimidin-5-yl) phenylsulfonyl]-4-methylpiperazine, better known as sildenafil which is the active ingredient in Viagra, Cialis, Revatio, Levitra, Vardenafil and any other boner building meds. One of the problems with sildenafil, especially for Malarkey, is that it doesn't work very well. Oh, he can get a semi-permanent erection, but it never seems to last and he always seems to get every other side effect, except the one he pines for: a four-hour hard on. As a way of sublimating, Malarkey has written a short story about sildenafil that the Reader will find at the end of this chapter.

At any rate, the morning after his Formula 1 orgasm, Malarkey slowly opens his eyes. Liliana fetchingly looks at him, her elbow on the bed, chin in hand and smiles a seductive smile.

"Morning, Humbert . . . wanna make a baby?"

At that hour, Malarkey isn't fully awake, but awake enough not to be seduced. He puts his finger in his ear as if he's not heard her correctly.

"Hmmm, not this morning, dear, but . . ."

"But what? But later?"

"No, but is breakfast included?"

Liliana shakes her head as if she's heard it all before. The woman is a saint. Who could possibly be with someone so incorrigible except, perhaps, Melania Trump. It is a testimony to her fortitude.

"You know, it's highly inappropriate for you to be sleeping with one of your advisees so if you don't want to be reported you should do as I ask."

"Yes, well, it's equally inappropriate for you to be abusing the elderly."

Liliana always sleeps in the nude. It's one of the many things that endears her to Malarkey since she's got a very 60s attitude to her body. She pulls back the sheets and straddles his chest. From Malarkey's point of view, she's a goddess: the brunette hair cascading across her shoulders and breasts, her Cupid's bow lips the envy of Venus herself; and he tries to reconcile why a goddess like Liliana would be straddling the geriatric chest of someone with solar lentigines and an occasional skin tag. If one believes in miracles in life then this straddling would be one of them.

"Is this elder abuse?"

"Without meds, yes, yes it is."

"Always an answer."

Liliana climbs out of bed and starts to walk toward the bathroom. Malarkey gazes at her from behind, lovely legs, pins of perfection, and a shapely ass meant for Ipanema. She looks over her shoulder and smiles as Malarkey turns to the Reader and raises his eyebrows as he is wont to do. If the Reader is finally realizing there may be a conflict between Liliana wanting a baby and Malarkey having second thoughts about creating one, then the Reader is not prescient, just able to read the obvious. To that end, Malarkey commends you. And now, this . . .

Osphena & Phil
-A Pre-Medicated Love Story-

Osphena Ospemifene (aka Οσφενα Οσπεμιφενε) and Phil Sildena met through an online dating site for people over fifty. Their exact ages are unimportant. What is important is that based on their profiles they seemed to have had multiple things in common. Lifestyle, background, education, interests, values, all those things that seem to make for an alleged match. Osphena was a seasoned traveler, had lived in France, Brazil and Argentina and was now divorced. She was a tall and slender woman, handsome in some respects, with a chiseled chin and brunette hair, with lips and eyewear not unlike Nana Mouskouri. As Phil was to discover, her name came from the Greek, Orchomenus, where she was born.

Phil was strapping for a man of his age, over six-feet tall and though his hair had receded long ago there were still some wisps of salt and pepper. His surname, "Silenda," was of Italian origins for those who came from Silendys which was once a part of Sondrio in Lombardy and which meant "to be silent." Like Osphena, Phil, too, was a seasoned traveler who, for a number of years, lived in both Nerja, in the south of Spain, as well as in Cassis, in the south of France. Like Osphena, he too was now divorced and was trying to begin afresh.

After emailing, texting and chatting for a couple of weeks they decided to meet for dinner. It took place in Manhattan Beach. *Il Fornaio*, as I recall. The sexual attraction was immediately palpable and the online photos did not belie her beauty, for she did, in fact, look like Nana Mouskouri. In between appetizers and entrées they chatted for hours about things like travel and children, food and film, art and music and everything seemed so right for the two of them. They talked for so long that they actually closed down the restaurant as the last two patrons to leave. Phil apologized profusely to the *maître'd* who merely replied, "È un piacere" and the two of them strolled out of the building. At some moment, their hands accidentally touched, then clasped until they reached her car and as he opened the door for her they kissed the first of would not be their last kiss.

For the next couple of weeks, they continued to Skype or email or chat on the phone; they dined at fashionable and not-so-fashionable eateries in Los Angeles and Orange County until the time came when Osphena, feeling totally comfortable with Phil, asked him if he would like to come for dinner. Of course, he couldn't refuse such a gracious

offer and so a date was set with all the attendant anxiet-
ies and reservations that would have accompanied such an
invitation.

As Phil was to discover, Osphena was a marvelous cook
who said she had once studied with the *maestro* himself,
Paul Bocuse, when she was living in Lyon with her ex-hus-
band who was a venture capitalist. Needless to say, Paul was
astonished to hear that and couldn't wait to see what kind of
a fantasy feast she would prepare for the two of them. Her
home was located in Pacific Palisades, perched on a bluff
overlooking the sea, and given the warmth of the July night,
they dined *al fresco* adjacent to the pool.

To say the very least, the dinner was magnificent and
would have made the *maestro* proud. For starters, scallop of
foie gras, pan-cooked, with a passion fruit sauce followed
by filet of beef Rossini and a Périgueux sauce with a side
of broccoli mousse. The feast was finished with fromage
blanc and double cream and consummately concluded with
a Sirio Crème brulée as only the *maestro* could have made
it. The dinner itself was companioned by more than one
bottle of Chateau Lafite Rothschild Pauillac, 1996 (which
Phil brought) and accompanied by selections from Jobim to
Veloso, Nascimento to Gilberto all of whom Osphena was
enamored based upon her lengthy sojourn in São Paulo.

The combination of dinner and wine and music went
delightfully to their heads and, needless to say, ended with
the inevitable voyage around her bedroom. As Osphena was
showing Phil some of the paintings she had acquired while
she lived in South America, she turned her back to him
and her tan shoulders and slender legs lasciviously exposed
beneath the little black dress was a bit too much for Phil to

handle and he brushed aside her shoulder-length hair and kissed the nape of her neck. There was no resistance. She excitedly turned. They kissed each other full on their mouths as they tumbled onto her bed.

Soon, their clothes were tossed, scattered on the hardwood floors, draped on the mid-eighteenth Century Venetian Commode and they began to kiss again, passionately. Hands and fingers and toes intermingled beneath the luxury of Sferra Egyptian cotton sheets and a Swedish comforter made in Malmö. As a super moon espied on them through French doors it seemed as if nothing in the world could undermine that exquisite moment, but when Phil placed his hand on her vagina, she suddenly stopped and bolted upright.

What's wrong? Phil asked. Did I do something wrong?

No, but I have something to tell you.

What is it?

She hesitated.

My gynecologist recommended that I pre-medicate.

For what?

She hesitated.

A dry vagina.

I see. And so? Is that a problem?

So, there might be some side effects.

Side effects? Like what?

Well, serious ones could include stroke or blood clots or eventually cancer of the lining of the uterus.

I see, but that's a worst-case scenario and they always have to say that in order to protect themselves legally.

Yes, I guess you're right.

She lay down again and they began intensely kissing, but

no sooner had they started when Osphena stopped again.

But there may be others.

Others? Really? Like what?

I could have unusual vaginal bleeding or there might be changes in my vision or speech.

Yes, but we'll just see what happens. Let's not get too alarmed about that right now.

You're right.

And they began kissing even more intensely than before, but once again Osphena stopped.

But there could be more.

How much more? Such as?

Such as sudden severe headaches or severe chest or leg pains. I might even have shortness of breath or sudden weakness and fatigue.

Certainly those things could be disarming, but we can monitor them. You know, just watch for them.

You're right.

And they began kissing again, but it wasn't long before Osphena curtailed their lovemaking.

But I could suffer from hot flashes or vaginal discharge or muscle spasms not to mention increased sweating. That would be so embarrassing.

Please, Osphena, there's nothing to be embarrassed about. That's all good to know, but let's just take our chances.

Yes, let's just take our chances, but truth is best.

Thanks for telling me.

Once again they began to kiss, passionately, but when Osphena reached for Phil's penis, he stopped abruptly.

What's wrong? Osphena asked. Did I do something wrong?

No, but I have something to tell you.

What is it?

He hesitated.

My urologist recommended that I pre-medicate.

For what?

He hesitated.

Erectile dysfunction.

I see. And so?

So, there might be some side effects.

Like what?

Well, serious ones could be hives or maybe difficulty in breathing. My face or my lips or tongue or throat even might swell.

I see, but that's a worst-case scenario and they always have to say that in order to protect themselves legally.

Yes, you're right.

And they began intensely kissing again, but no sooner had they started than Phil stopped.

But there may be others.

Others? Really? Like what?

During sex, I might get dizzy or nauseated, or have pain, or numbness or tingling in my chest, arms, neck, or jaw as if I were having a heart attack.

Certainly, those things could be disarming, but we can monitor them. You know, just watch for them.

Yes, you're right.

And they initiated the kissing once again, but it wasn't long before Phil curtailed the lovemaking.

If that happens, I'd have to stop and call my doctor right away. And that would be so embarrassing.

Please, Phil, there's nothing to be embarrassed about.

I understand and, if that happens, we'll call immediately.

Seemingly relaxed, they started what they had started numerous times before, but, once again, no sooner had they started when Phil abruptly quit.

But I could suddenly go blind or deaf not to mention vomiting and sweating along with an irregular heartbeat. I just had to tell you everything. Truth is best.

Thank you. That's all good to know, said Osphena, but let's take our chances. Try to relax.

And they endeavored to begin again, but no sooner had they started when Phil stopped one last time.

But, and this is the worst of all, I could have a painful erection or that might last for four hours. Maybe longer.

She hesitated.

And that would be the worst of all? She asked quizzically.

I just can't imagine having an erection for four hours, can you?

Osphena raised her eyebrows, but said nothing.

And I couldn't imagine having a dry vagina for four hours, can you?

Phil raised his eyebrows, but said nothing.

For the next twenty minutes the two potential lovers lie in bed, fingers folded on their respective chests, staring at the ceiling or gazing at the super moon beyond the French doors when Osphena turned to Phil and Phil turned to Osphena and together they said, "Maybe this isn't such a good idea."

Yes, you're probably right, they responded in unison and after the two of them got dressed, they shared a cognac, and kissed goodnight. Phil drove home to Villa Park. They never met again, and what could have perhaps become a relationship for the ages, merely ended as it had begun:

an online date pre-medicated for Osphena Ospemifene and Phil Sildena.

Just why Malarkey included this short story isn't very clear. Perhaps, in a way, it was a way of avoiding baby talk, but that, like the length of time sildenafil works, won't last.

CHAPTER TWENTY-NINE

WHEN YOU ARE OLD AND GRAY

Later that day, Malarkey and Liliana walk along Carmel Beach, holding hands. Now, for those Readers who have not walked Carmel Beach holding hands or not, then nothing Malarkey can write would be good enough to describe it. Comprehend it. Neither an Ansel Adams photo nor an R. L. Stevenson narrative passage could do justice to walks on the seashell white sands of Carmel Beach, as the Pacific fog passively creeps in before seducing the shoreline. It's December, the water's cold, but they walk barefoot anyway, holding their shoes in their hands. Malarkey walks Liliana toward a sand dune and they sit beneath a cypress overlooking the soon to be sequestered shore. Malarkey has no intention of writing about cypress trees and how, in classical antiquity, they were a symbol of mourning and so he leaves it at that. Malarkey leans back against the tree as Liliana sits between his legs. He wraps his arms around her as they both look out to sea.

"One day, twenty-five years ago, I came here to get away from academics. From grading papers and attending meetings and dealing with the bureaucracy, with the onslaught of memos and meaningless messages about minutiae. From students pleading for direction their parents avoided giving them."

"Did it help?"

"I wasn't here but for a day when my mother called to tell me my father died of cancer. And I remember I came to this tree, sat down and wept."

Liliana says nothing, just holds his hands closer to her stomach.

"He was a self-learner. Never finished high school. When I was accepted to Oxford, there wasn't a soul he didn't tell. And when he died, a copy of my first novel was on his nightstand. The day before my father died, the attending physician saw the book, showed it to him and asked him if he recognized the author. According to my mother, my father merely scowled at him as if in some small, defiant measure he was politely telling the physician to fuck off. It was his last scowl, but I can imagine what it looked like and six weeks later, almost to the day, my mother died."

Malarkey pauses for a moment and gathers his thoughts.

"When you are old and gray and full of sleep, And nodding by the fire, take down this book, And slowly read, and dream of the soft look Your eyes had once, and of their shadows deep; How many loved your moments of glad grace, And loved your beauty with love false or true, But one man loved the pilgrim Soul in you, And loved the sorrows of your changing face; And bending down beside the glowing bars, Murmur, a little sadly, how Love fled And paced upon the mountains overhead And hid his face amid a crowd of stars."

"Yeats."

"Yeats."

"How did she die?"

"Doc said it was an aneurysm, but I'm convinced it was from reading my last unpublished novel."

Liliana turns to look at Malarkey, at Malarkey with the bittersweet smile.

"I love you, Malarkey."

Malarkey looks at her, there's a pause.

"When I die I want your name to be the last name on my lips."

She kisses him on the lips and as they walk hand in hand through Carmel listening to the senescent sounds of the sea from somewhere in that cloudless sunset they faintly hear the song "The Folks Who Live On The Hill" which fittingly ends as they approach the Café Carmel.

Things seem to be getting a bit too maudlin here what with death and dying and Yeats and weeping, so Malarkey thinks it best to move on with the plot and after they leave the beach, they go to the Café Carmel. This is the inside of the Café Carmel:

They order two cappuccinos.

"Have you decided what you want to do after finals?" Liliana asks.

"Probably stay home and make a futile attempt at finishing a futile novel. The futility of it all. I feel as if I were a piece in a game of chess, when my opponent says of it: that piece cannot be moved and if you move it wherever you move it you're checked."

"That's not Yeats."

"Kierkegaard."

"How's Italy sound to you?"

"As a culture or an investment?"

"I'm going home for the holidays and I want you to come with me."

"To meet the Fockers?"

"In a way."

"How do you think that'll work out?"

"Trust me. It'll work out fine."

"Based on what you've told me about them, especially about your mother, I'm not so sure."

"They're my parents and I'll deal with them."

She looks at her engagement ring.

"What do I do in the meantime?"

"In the meantime, try to pack as if you were going for more than a weekend. Or do you want me to do it?"

"No, I can do it. Just need to buy some new blue work shirts."

"Precisely."

"Not sure I want to leave Carmel."

"Why not?"

"Because . . ."

"Because you'll have to finish grading final exams from nineteen-ninety?"

"You know me so well."

"You have no idea how well. No idea."

They kiss. End of chapter.

CHAPTER THIRTY

A FORMULA IN WHICH
THE PLOT THICKENS

After Malarkey and Liliana return from Carmel, she spends the night at his place. What happens that night is irrelevant. What happens the following morning is. Liliana sits on the toilet and as she does, she notices a small, white, freestanding medicine cabinet with glass panes. She opens the doors of the cabinet and discovers a prescription bottle of sildenafil in front of an unused plastic specimen bottle. The specimen bottle has the name, MALCOLM MALARKEY and beneath it, SEMEN ANALYSIS, DR. BAKO and beneath that the date of OCTOBER 15. Liliana thoughtfully closes the cabinet doors; however, the expression on her face registers disappointment. If the Reader cannot understand her disappointment, then, in some ways, the Reader is very much like Malarkey. In that case, there is not much hope for either of you.

CHAPTER THIRTY-ONE

THE STATE OF EDUCATION AS IT SOMETIMES IS

It's a few days later. There are Christmas decorations and lights on the façade of Morbittity Hall. Inside, Malarkey sits at a desk at the front of the classroom as students finish their final exam. He looks up at the clock. The clock reads noon.

"Time's up. Stack your finals here," he says.

One by one, the students pass his desk and pile their blue books one on top of another. Wilson is no exception.

"Nailed it, prof."

"Brilliant. Couldn't be happier."

Later that afternoon, as Malarkey attempts to grade those finals, a chore that only reminds him of the fact that reading anything longer than a tweet has become tantamount to translating Tolstoy into Aramaic, there's a knock at his door. Malarkey reluctantly gets out of his chair and opens the door. It's a student he doesn't recognize holding a blue book in his hands. At first, Malarkey squints, thinking to himself, "Who is this unknown fellow with a blue book in his hands? And why is he here standing with a blue book in his hands?"

"Professor Malarkey?"

Malarkey opens the door and traces his finger across his nameplate.

"My name is Randle McMurphy."

Malarkey clearly knows who Randle McMurphy is; he wrinkles his brow, but doesn't let on. Sometimes, students believe professors only have one life to live and that one life is in the classroom after which they climb into a cardboard box and await the next time they have to teach, climb out of the box, and begin the exercise once again. The use of the name Randle McMurphy is a testimony to that ignorant perception.

"Not _the_ Randle McMurphy?"

"Uh, yes."

"I see. So, what can I do for you . . . Randle McMurphy?"

"I just finished taking a final exam in Morbittity Hall and found this blue book on the floor." Malarkey looks at the name on the blue book. "Wade Wilson must have dropped it by accident," McMurphy offers.

"Of course, by accident. Well, thank you, Randle. I'm extremely appreciative. This will make all the difference in the world to Wilson's grade."

"Yes, that's what I thought. Well, thank you, professor."

"No, thank _you_ for bringing this to my attention."

Malarkey takes the blue book, closes the door and walks to his desk.

"Randle fucking McMurphy. Must have dropped it by accident. McMurphy my ass."

He rummages through the pile of finals looking for

Wilson's other blue book, finds it and smiles. After Malarkey reads the final exam, he emails Wilson and asks him to come to his office where the latter appears to be somewhat nervous, fidgeting in his seat.

"Let's talk final exams," Malarkey begins.

"I nailed it, sir."

"You certainly did, Wilson, you certainly did. It seems you dropped one of your blue books when you turned in the final exam and another student, a Mr. McMurphy, was kind enough to bring it to me."

"Phew! Thanks for letting me know. I'm glad he found it. That could have been a disaster, sir. Is that why I'm here?"

"No, Wilson, actually the reason you're here is because, well, you cheated."

"Cheated?"

"Yes, Wilson, cheated. You see, I know your itty bitty scam."

"Scam? What scam?"

"Wilson, do you know how some pickpockets work in teams?"

"Not really."

"Let me enlighten you, in case you want to take up pick-pocketing as a profession after being dismissed from university. You see, your friend, Randle McMurphy, is part of your team."

"What do you mean?"

Malarkey gets annoyed.

"Don't take me for a fool, Wilson. You wrote the last sentence of your answer to the last question in blue book number two, went home, copied the answers to all the questions into blue book number one and then had your McMurphy goon deliver it, didn't you?"

"No, I, uh, have no idea what you're talking about. I expected to do well."

"Yes, well, expectation is the mother of all sorrow."

"I studied hard for the final."

"No, Wilson, you studied hard to figure out how to cheat, which will get you an 'F' on the exam and an 'F' in the course. You can appeal my decision if you want, but right now we're finished."

"But . . ."

"No buts, Wilson. Please leave. I'll report this to the Chancellor's office."

Wilson starts to leave.

"Oh, and one more thing."

Wilson turns.

"When you see McMurphy, tell him I loved him in *Five Easy Pieces*."

Wilson nods and leaves the office. Malarkey turns to the Reader.

"Now, you might think Wilson was expelled for flagrant cheating. An egregious act beyond egregious acts. But, you see, Wilson's father is a major donor to the university and, well, the sons of major donors may one day become major donors themselves, so Wilson was merely put on probation for one semester and could retake the course to eliminate the "F." Life in the academy. So it goes."

At that point, Malarkey gets a text message from Liliana:

Lunch?

Who's paying?

You are?

I'll meet you at the trolley stop.

Malarkey and Liliana stop next to the Citrus City College

Trolley. It's not a trolley *per se*, but it's in the style of a San Francisco trolley with the difference being the trolley doesn't run on rails, but on tires. On the front and sides of the fire engine red trolley, the name CITRUS CITY COLLEGE TROLLEY appears in gold, Italianate letters. People climb on.

"Let's take this to the café for lunch," Malarkey says.

"It's only a few blocks. We can walk."

"C'mon. Never rode this before."

So, Malarkey and Liliana climb on. There are students seated next to them and a few faculty members.

"Would everyone please buckle up?" the driver asks.

The riders put on their seat belts, as does Liliana, but Malarkey doesn't.

"Sir, would you kindly put on your seat belt?"

"Why?"

"College policy."

"That's okay, I'll take my chances."

"Please, just buckle up."

"You're kidding, right? This bloody thing travels at ten miles an hour for four blocks. Who needs a seat belt?"

The Reader has to imagine what transpires due to Malarkey's obstinacy since the trolley driver has no option but to call the police and before Malarkey knows it, there's a half-dozen Citrus City campus and city police cars surrounding the trolley. A swat team stands on top of the trolley, masked and in armor, with assault rifles drawn. One can hear a police helicopter whirling above with Malarkey on the ground, hands behind his back, cuffed as Marvin Gaye sings, "What's Going On." Malarkey looks at the Reader straining to lift his head and barely mumbles . . .

"Can I get a witness?"

CHAPTER THIRTY-TWO

THE CHANCELLOR SPEAKS

"Malcolm, you can't do that."

CHAPTER THIRTY-THREE

IF THOUGHTS WERE THINGS, THEN MALARKEY WOULD HAVE BEEN SACKED & AN UNEXPECTED VISITOR

Starbucks has a café located on the Citrus City campus and Malarkey stands in line to buy a Caramel Brulée Latte. It's Christmas time, but in Citrus City the weather never changes so it would be hard to tell without the Christmas baubles. Global warming doesn't exist in a globally warm climate, so denial is a way of life. Standing behind him is a lovely young woman about twenty years old, with long blonde hair and blue eyes, who's wearing very short cut-off jeans and a flimsy halter-top that exposes most of her nubile breasts. Malarkey moves up a bit more in line, but the line is somewhat long so he's not at the register yet. In the meantime, he turns and looks behind him and pretends he's looking for someone when, in fact, he just wants to get a better look at the co-ed's fulsome breasts. Malarkey turns back toward the register, but the line still isn't moving very fast. He turns again toward the co-ed who's so absorbed in scrolling through her cell phone that she has no clue as to what Malarkey is doing. Then, suddenly, without notice, Malarkey turns, pulls the halter top down and cups both hands around her breasts to see what kind of reaction he gets. The co-ed, absorbed as she is in scrolling through her cell phone, doesn't react at all, but if thoughts were things then Malarkey would have been sacked on the spot.

But fortunately, for Malarkey, thoughts are not things and Malarkey returns to his office to pick up a few things before their trip. Waiting in the hall is Matthew who, from the looks of it, is preoccupied.

"Matthew. How are you?"

"Fine. Do you have a moment?"

"Of course."

They enter Malarkey's office.

"Have a seat? What's up? Ready for break?"

Matthew sits down. He's obviously grappling with something and is trying not to become emotional. Malarkey sees what he's going through, leans forward and taps him on the thigh.

"What is it, Matthew? Are you okay?"

Matthew nods without looking.

"Take your time."

"I'm struggling."

"With what? Certainly not your studies."

"No, my . . . sexuality." Malarkey pauses for a moment realizing he needs to focus.

"I see. What about it?"

"I'm . . . gay."

Malarkey is unfazed by the comment. It's not as if he's had a lot of experience with this sort of thing, but enough to know it's a major moment in Matthew's life if not Malarkey's.

"And?"

"And I'm not sure how to tell my parents."

"What do you think will happen if you tell them?"

"I'm not sure."

"What's the worst case?"

"They'll be upset. Shocked, disappointed, angry. Especially my father."

"And not your mother?"

"No, maybe her too, but he's . . ."

"He's what?"

"He's very religious, a man of God and I'm not sure he'll understand."

"Matthew, I can't tell you the best way to tell your folks, but this is what I can tell you." He leans close to him. "You have nothing to feel shameful or guilty about. Your sexual orientation does not define you as a human being. Our identities are shaped by what we do in our lives and how we deal with other people and I can tell you this . . . you are an exceptional human being. You need to pick a time that's good for you. Perhaps, a place and tell them what you're feeling. You can do no more."

Matthew keeps his emotions under wraps and nods his head.

"Thank you for your time."

"No, thank you for coming to me. I feel privileged that you would do so and don't hesitate to talk to me whenever you feel like it."

Matthew gets up as does Malarkey. Matthew starts to leave, turns and hugs Malarkey who embraces him as his own. Malarkey has some difficulty controlling his emotions as well since more than anything else, Malarkey tries to hide those things. After all, he's a professor.

CHAPTER THIRTY-FOUR

PRELUDE TO THE AFTERNOON OF A FLIGHT

The Reader has the option of reading this chapter to the music of Debussy's *Prélude à l'après-midi d'un faune*, or not, as it will have no impact on the outcome of the chapter whatsoever. Once again, Malarkey helps you out: (https://www.youtube.com/watch?v=Ol4bSKpvpoc). As you listen to this music, the following conversation takes place between Liliana and Malarkey. Imagine you see them from a helicopter as they ride in a shuttle heading to LAX. The dialogue before their flight might have gone something like this:

"Coach? I'm not flying coach to Milan," Liliana says.

"But just think how snug we'll be."

"Snug or no snug, no way."

"Well, Andrea's ticket pretty much did me in. No help from mom."

"I'll pay for half your ticket."

"Really? I've never flown business."

"Consider it a Christmas present."

"How can I ever repay you?'

"Don't worry, I'll think of something."

And the Reader is probably thinking the same thing.

END PART I

ACT II

ON THE SHORES OF LAGO MAGGIORE

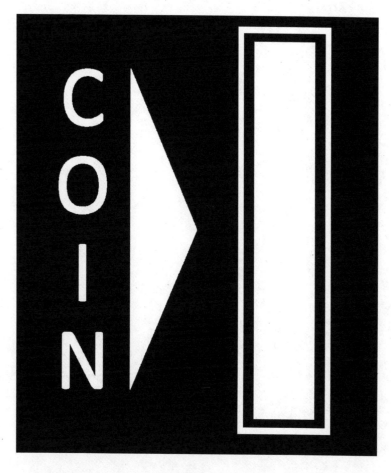

Malarkey is tired of writing for nothing. He's been writing for nothing for decades and, frankly, he's fed up with it. To read on, please insert 10 silver dollars in the slot. Thank you. You may now turn the page.

"Ever tried. Ever failed. No matter. Try Again. Fail again. Fail better."

—Samuel Beckett

CHAPTER THIRTY-FIVE

THE MILE HIGH CLUB;
OR, TRICKED OR TREATED: PART II

Malarkey and Liliana are flying business class on KLM. They would have taken Alitalia, but Liliana never liked flying Alitalia since it's run by Italians. Most of the passengers are asleep so the lights are off except for one or two passengers who think they won't suffer from a lack of sleep upon landing; however, Malarkey and Liliana are reading. Malarkey is reading García Márquez's *One Hundred Years of Solitude* (no irony where none intended) while Liliana continues reading her Virginia Woolf collection. Specifically, "The Nail on the Wall" which, given her circumstances is an appropriate story to read. "The Yellow Wallpaper" is a close second. Now while Liliana reads, Malarkey has an idea. Malarkey often has ideas when he flies and, generally, they are bad ideas. Perhaps, it's the elevation that affects his thinking. Then again, it might be they are bad ideas to begin with. After all, Malarkey is often delusional. This particular idea is a novel one for Malarkey in that he's often thought about the idea, but has never put it into practice. In other words, up until this time it's just been a theory. As theories go, some are predicated on research, others, not so much. If the Reader is a Marxist, think of it as praxis.

Anyway, Malarkey puts down his book and whispers in Liliana's ear. Even though he whispers, the Reader can hear him whisper because Malarkey is now whispering to the Reader what he's whispering to Liliana. What a concept.

"You a member?"

"Of what? The frequent flyer club?"

"No, the mile high club."

"No, why?"

"You wanna join?"

"Are you kidding?" Liliana says, squinting.

"No."

"You're serious?"

"Yes."

Liliana thinks about it for a moment, as she's not forgotten the horrors of Halloween, but being the intrepid Italian she is and since she loves Malarkey, she agrees. After all, what can possibly go wrong with one of Malarkey's ideas?

"Okay."

"Brilliant."

"Now what?"

"You go first."

"And?"

"And a few minutes later I'll knock three times."

Liliana squints at him.

"How Bond of you."

"So, what are you wearing?" he asks, raising his eyebrows.

"It's 'Risky.'"

"Why's it risky?"

"I don't know. That's what they call it."

"No, not your perfume your, you know . . ."

"They're called thongs, Malcolm."

Malarkey raises his eyebrows.

"Right. Take them off now. It'll be easier."

"You're insane, you know that?"

"Yes, but sanity is such a poor alternative."

She wriggles out of her thong and dangles it in his face.

"Now what? James?"

He waves her off.

"Go, go."

She slides out of her seat, walks to the toilet, and not without a soupçon of trepidation looks back at him before she walks in. The flight attendants are either asleep or preoccupied with other things like complaining about passengers who complain about flight attendants or the quality of food or the smell of other passengers silently farting *ad astra*. So they're not paying any attention. Malarkey waits for a short time, walks to the toilet and quietly taps three times. Liliana slowly opens the door and he squeezes in. It's been said the best predictor of future behavior is past behavior and nowhere is that more applicable than with Malarkey who, because of the cramped quarters, once again forgets to do what he should remember to do; namely, lock the door.

Now, unbeknownst to either Malarkey or Liliana or the Reader for that matter, Chancellor Jones is flying first class on the same KLM flight. Why he's flying on the same flight will become apparent upon landing, but at that moment all the Reader needs to know is the Chancellor has an urge to pee. After all, when one can drink as much Barolo as one wishes on first class, frequent urination is axiomatic. However, he notices the toilets in first class are occupied presumably by other Barolo drinkers so he walks down the stairs to use the toilets in business class. After all, if one flies first class then one is entitled to use any lavatory one desires. Such privileges come with the fare. Since the lavatory in which Malarkey and Liliana are currently engaged is unlocked, the lavatory sign naturally reads "unoccupied" so Jones feels comfortable just walking in, which he does. From his point of view, Jones sees Liliana sitting on the edge of the washbasin with her legs wrapped around Malarkey's waist, which, as the Reader knows, is not the first time she's had her legs wrapped about his waist in a lavatory. As recidivism would have it, Liliana looks up horrified, but, as usual, Malarkey takes it all in stride: "Keep calm and carry on," being one of his slogans.

"Chancellor, fancy meeting you here. So, how's the flight?"

CHAPTER THIRTY-SIX

THE MORNING AFTER THE NIGHT BEFORE; OR, DEALING WITH YOUR BAGGAGE AT MALPENSA

There's little need to go into what transpired immediately after Jones discovered them *in flagrante delicto* in the lavatory. One can only imagine. What are the odds? Even in fiction. However, during the remainder of the flight Liliana says not a word to Malarkey. Not a single word. Oh, she thinks of lots of things to say, especially in Italian, the language of choice when one is pissed beyond normal rhetoric. But she doesn't. For example, she might want to say: "Non capisco un cavolo!" or "Non rompermi i coglioni!" or "Vai a farti fottere!" But she doesn't. She must save that for a later time, but at the moment, her silence is as obscene as if she were to say: "Non capisco un cavolo!" or "Non rompermi i coglioni!" or "Vai a farti fottere!"

The Reader might think she's keeping it all inside until they land. If that's what the Reader might think, then the Reader would be completely correct. Needless to say, because of the interruption, Liliana is only partially inducted

into the Mile High Club and if past behavior is a predictor
of future behavior then the Reader will not be surprised by
what happens when they arrive at Milan's Malpensa Airport
as Malarkey and Liliana wait for their luggage. It's beyond
clear that Liliana is more than a bit agitated about the nightmare that was the night before as she reads Malarkey the
"riot act." Although the actual Riot Act of 1714 declared any
group of twelve or more people to be unlawfully assembled,
and thus have to disperse or face punitive action has absolutely nothing to do with Liliana's anger, the Reader should
get the drift here. If not, Malarkey isn't going to explain it
to you, but after she uses the words she thought about using
the night before; namely, "Non capisco un cavolo!" or "Non
rompermi i coglioni!" or "Vai a farti fottere!" things don't
improve.

"How could you be so stupid as to not lock the door!"
Liliana screams in the clearest of all possible English.

There's little need for a dialogue tag here. If the Reader
can't imagine how pissed off she is, a dialogue tag won't
help.

"Jesus. It was cramped. I'm not Houdini!"

"You don't need to be Houdini to lock the damn door!
How incredibly embarrassing!" Liliana sticks two fingers
in Malarkey's face. "Twice! It's happened twice! Have you
lost your memory?"

Malarkey shrugs his shoulders and raises his eyebrows
as if it's not out of the realm of possibility that someone his
age might, in fact, be losing his memory since Malarkey's
been losing his memory for years as the Reader may recall
from the house key fiasco. As a matter of fact, losing his
memory has bailed Malarkey out of a number of situations

in which losing one's memory is the response of choice.

For the Reader's edification, as we age there are physiological changes in brain function that can create difficulties in recalling short-term information. In fact, this slowing of mental processes is not really memory loss, but failing to remember. For the Reader's edification, as we age there are physiological changes in brain function that can create difficulties in recalling short-term information. In fact, this slowing of mental processes is not really memory loss, but failing to remember. For the Reader's edification, as we age there are physiological changes in brain function that can create difficulties in recalling short-term information. In fact, this slowing of mental processes is not really memory loss, but failing to remember. Regardless, Malarkey thinks carefully about her statement then attempts to mollify her in the most banal of ways.

"But good things come in pairs, honey bunch."

"Shut up! Don't honey bunch me! I can't believe I listened to you!"

"Let's think about this rationally, sweetheart. How would I know the Chancellor was married to an Italian and was flying first class on a bloody Dutch airline to visit in-laws in Milan? What are the odds!"

"He must think I'm a slut."

"Probably, but you're my slut."

He tries to put his arm around her, but she's too pissed off and pushes him away.

"Why'd I listen to you?"

"C'mon, Luciana."

If the Reader is a perspicacious Reader (and does not need to look up the word "perspicacious," which would

retard the read) then the Reader remembers "Luciana" is
not Liliana's name, but the name of Malarkey's ex-wife.
This "player error" is something that many ex-husbands
are wont to do and the results of such errors can be fatal.
This player error is exacerbated if the ex has a name that's
similar to the name of the newly beloved; in this case . . .
Liliana-Luciana. Both with three syllables. It's a simple
mistake, but, as Malarkey says, as simple mistakes go it
can be lethal. Many an ex has found himself masturbat-
ing on the living room couch for months because of such
a player error. Just why this Freudian mistake happens
is one of the mysteries of the universe, along with Black
Holes, Dark Energy, String Theory, parallel universes, frac-
tals, and aliens in Nevada, but suffice to say, it does not go
over well with Liliana. In Malarkey's defense, Malarkey's
Theory of Unrequited Angles has some measure. Before
Liliana and after Luciana there were a number of women
Malarkey dated all of whom had first names with the letter
"L"; the blonde television anchor, Loretta, who would go
into a frenzy at the mere mention of the word "anus"; the
Italian restauranteur, Leonora, who would smear herself in
brie (camembert if brie were unavailable) and ask Malarkey
to lick it off; the Harley aficionado, Lisa, who could only
make love to one of her 1,000 LPs; the watercolorist, Lani,
who could only have sex after she was thoroughly painted
in such; and the bisexual academic, Louisa, who instructed
Malarkey in the fine art of cunnilingus, so, one might be
willing to excuse Malarkey for incorrectly calling Liliana,
Luciana. Then again, it just might be a lame excuse.

   "What did you call me?" Liliana asks, questioning
whether she hears Malarkey correctly.

Malarkey realizes the gaffe, but any man worthy of calling himself a man, Alpha or otherwise, would never admit to the mistake and fall back on the heretofore-mentioned memory loss.

"Call you? Call you? I didn't call you anything, honey bunch."

"Did you just call me, Luciana?"

Malarkey shifts into a combination of memory loss and "stupid mode." Stupid mode is a well-known mode for men who, when caught with their pants down (literally or figuratively) rely on stupidity for survival. It works well with memory loss, especially if one is over sixty-five. This does not work well if one is only fifty, to which Malarkey can attest. It's a bit like having a really good back-up quarterback.

"Don't think so. I'd certainly remember if I called you that. Wow."

Liliana sticks the finger of little misunderstanding in his face.

"You listen to me carefully! Call me Luciana one more time, just one more time and you won't be traveling with anyone . . . ever. Luciana my ass!"

Malarkey tries to put his arm around her again, but she flips it off.

"That's just the jet lag talking, honey bunch," he says trying to dismiss her comment.

"No, that's *Li-li-ana* talking!"

"Sorry. Haven't traveled with a woman in a while."

"That's so lame, Malcolm. Get the goddamn bags!"

With the help of a baggage handler, they walk outside with their luggage on a cart at which time they're met by Mario who's in his early fifties and dressed in the livery of a chauffeur. Malarkey is a bit puzzled by his presence since Mario seems to be on familiar terms with Liliana. Though their conversation is in Italian, Malarkey has translated it for you.

"Welcome, Miss Liliana. Good to have you home."

"Nice to be back. Mario, this is Malcolm."

"My pleasure."

"Grazie."

Mario takes the cart and they walk toward the parking lot. Mario opens the doors of a newly waxed, jet-black, Bentley "Flying Spur" as Malarkey and Liliana climb into the back seat, before he places the luggage in the trunk and climbs behind the wheel. It's got all the "bells and whistles" a Bentley costing $250,000 could possibly have and Malarkey is impressed by it.

"Are you comfortable?" Mario asks.

"Who wouldn't be?"

Malarkey turns to Liliana.

"What kind of a shuttle service is this where you're on a first name basis with the driver?" he whispers.

"It's not a shuttle service, Malcolm. Mario's our chauffeur."

Malarkey thinks she's joking.

"Oh, our chauffeur. And I'm Bond, James Bond."

She doesn't respond, which gives Malarkey pause.

"Uh, you're serious. You never told me . . ."

"Nothing to tell. Enjoy the ride."

Her pissed-offed-ness is slowly waning thanks to the jet lag rather than anything Malarkey has said or done. As Mario drives off and after a few moments of silence, Malarkey feels compelled to speak.

"About the club . . . "

"Don't want to talk about it."

"I'm sorry. Wasn't thinking."

"You rarely do. It's one of your virtues . . . but I agreed to do it."

"Still love me?"

"Jury's out . . . maybe later."

She puts her arm beneath his, rests her head on his shoulder, closes her eyes, and falls sleep.

CHAPTER THIRTY-SEVEN

AT THE VILLA LILIANO

After leaving the airport, Mario heads toward Arona, which is about an hour outside of Milan: forty-two miles or sixty-eight kilometers depending on whether you're an American or not. Malarkey absorbs the scenery, and continues stroking Liliana's hair even though she's already fallen asleep. Before long, they arrive in Arona on the shores of Lake Maggiore. Malarkey could describe Lake Maggiore perhaps in the manner of Thomas Mann. But Malarkey isn't Thomas Mann; however, if he were Thomas Mann he might describe what he sees in the following manner:

Malarkey looks out the Bentley window. Water roars in the abysses on the right; on the left among rocks, dark fir-trees aspire toward a bluish sky, silent scuttering of stratus clouds. A magnificent succession of vistas open before Malarkey's eyes, of the solemn, almost phantasmagorical world of towering snowscaped peaks, into which their route might weave and worm itself. New vistas appear and disappear with each new winding of the road. Malarkey reflects that they must have got above the zone of shade-trees, also probably of song-birds; whereupon he feels such a sense of the impoverishment of life as to give him a slight attack of giddiness and nausea and make him put his hand over his eyes for a few seconds. It passes. The lake is visible in the distant landscape, its waters a chilling blue, its shores covered with black fir-forests that climb the surrounding heights, thinned out, and give place to bare, mist-wreathed rock. Beyond the lake, the Alps, the snow-peaked mountain massif Monte Rosa, peers down upon the lake, upon Locarno and Stresa and Arona. It is here where Malarkey and Liliana are headed, but for what purpose even Thomas Mann is unclear.

But since Malarkey isn't Thomas Mann, Malarkey circumvents such a description this way:

Now you get the picture. The Villa Liliano is a magnificent nineteenth-century estate, which sits on a promontory overlooking Lago Maggiore on the other side of Arona. Mario drives through the monogramed silver gates and down the circuitous lane that is sheltered by looming pines, the tips of which have created a kind of canopy due to the Mistral-like winds that skirt the surface of Lago Maggiore in the winter. And then, suddenly, this:

As the Reader can see, it's a visual feast cradled as it is with its own forest of chestnut and plane trees, palm trees and cypresses. The estate was once owned by the Viscount Medardo of Terralba, a distant relative of the novelist Italo Calvino. But its history is unimportant. What is important, is that standing outside is Liliana's father, Giancarlo Liliano, who's in his late sixties. Giancarlo looks so much like Giancarlo Giannini he could actually be Giancarlo Giannini so the Reader should imagine him being Giancarlo Giannini dressed in a handmade blue pinstripe suit and matching tie. He is reserved by nature, but as he stands with his hands behind his back, the Reader notices that despite his reserved nature, he's eager to see his daughter. As Mario removes the luggage, Malarkey turns to Mario and says in Italian:

"How do you like driving this beauty?"

Mario smiles and responds.

"It is better than sex, signore."

"Maybe I should try it. You think I could?" he whispers to Mario.

"If it is fine with Signore Liliano I do not see why not."

Malarkey raises his eyebrows. Liliana grabs her purse from the trunk.

"You never told me you spoke Italian."

"It's pigeon Italian."

He smiles. Signore Liliano approaches them.

"My love."

He hugs and kisses Liliana.

"Papa, this is Malcolm."

Signore Liliano holds out his hand and smiles broadly.

"My pleasure."

"Pleasure is all mine."

"I imagine the both of you are quite tired, no? Would you like to rest?"

"Yes, I'll take Malcolm to my room. Where's mother?"

"Your mother is resting. She'll join us for sherry before dinner."

"Of course," Liliana answers as if that's routine for her mother.

They start to walk inside.

"After you," says Signore Liliano.

"No, after you."

Signore Liliano is seemingly impressed with Malarkey's protocol if not his novice language skills since the entire conversation is in Italian, but since Malarkey can't assume the reader reads Italian he's written it in English.

"But of course."

As the Reader can imagine, the interior of Villa Liliano is an opulent nineteenth-century home whose massive living room windows overlook the lake. Classic furniture that could be out of a showroom at Sotheby's infects the entire house; eighteenth and nineteenth -century oil paintings are

strategically arranged on the walls; there's an original nineteenth Century Italian Gothic Travertine fireplace above
which hangs a six-foot oil portrait of a standing Signora
Liliano, a septuagenarian, seventy to be exact, who appears
to be looking down at the viewer with a somewhat disdainful gaze. She seems to be the quintessential matriarch:
blond, statuesque; regal, very Jane Fonda-like. Actually,
she looks so much like Jane Fonda she could actually be
Jane Fonda so think of Jane Fonda as you read this chapter.
Next to the floor-to-ceiling windows stands an elaborately
decorated ten-foot Christmas tree strangely bereft of gifts.
Hands clasped behind his back, Malarkey looks at Signora
Liliano's portrait as if it were something out of the Tate.

"My, my, my. Beautiful portrait."

"Yes, my wife. Painted by a relative of Modigliani.
Please, rest. Mario will bring your luggage upstairs."

Malarkey and Liliana both start up the elegantly balus-
traded stairs. As Signore Liliano watches them ascend the
staircase, Malarkey turns.

"Should I wear a suit to dinner?" he half-jokingly asks.

"No, a sport coat and tie will be fine."

Signore Liliano walks away as Malarkey furrows his
brow and follows Liliana upstairs to her bedroom, which
is as expansive as, and not unlike, the style of the living
room, classically decorated with tall windows that overlook
the lake. There are relics of her childhood appropriately
displayed on mantels and windowsills, on walls and tables,
such as the Brevi and Faro toys from the 80s. It appears
as if little has changed since she left Arona. Perhaps, it's a
way for Liliana to remember herself as a child. Perhaps, it's
a way for Signora Liliano to remember her daughter as a

child. Or to treat her as one. Regardless, Malarkey takes off his shoes and plops on the California king-size bed.

"That went over swimmingly, don't you think?"

"As you may have noticed he's somewhat reserved."

"Reserved? Your father? Really?"

"Don't be an ass."

"Why go out of character."

Liliana doesn't respond.

"By the way, I was kidding about the suit," Malarkey says.

"Well, he wasn't kidding about the sport coat and tie. I hope you brought a clean shirt."

There's a knock at the door. She opens it and Mario brings in the suitcases.

"Just over there, Mario. Grazie mille."

Mario puts them in a corner and leaves.

"Prego."

Liliana walks into the *en suite* bathroom, hikes up her skirt, pulls down her panties and sits on the toilet. Malarkey looks her way.

"Somehow an open door policy here seems strangely out of place," Malarkey says. "Almost as if one should have permission to urinate. Which reminds me. What kind of royal toilet paper do you think the Queen uses?"

Liliana ignores him, finishes her business, flushes the toilet and washes her hands.

"Get over it."

She climbs on the bed next him.

"So, where's mommy?"

"Mother rarely greets anyone at the door."

"Even you?"

"Even me. When she's ready, my father will escort us to her."

Malarkey squints as if he heard her incorrectly.

"Escort us? Like with bodyguards and shit? Don't tell me your mother is a princess, too?"

"What do you mean, 'too'? Are you implying . . ."

"No, just seems a bit odd to me that we'd need to be escorted downstairs to see your mother. Nice tree though. Where are the presents?"

"There aren't any."

"Because?"

"Because she doesn't believe in giving presents."

"So, why the tree?"

"She believes in the spirit of the holiday."

"So do I, but I can still splurge at Target once a year."

"Listen, Malcolm," Liliana begins seriously. "I know how you can be, so please try your best to be polite."

"I'll be on my best behavior. Which is dicey indeed."

Liliana snuggles next to him and closes her eyes. Malarkey strokes her hair, but doesn't sleep. He gazes out the window. From Malarkey's point of view, he sees the afternoon light fade slowly into darkness. Across the lake, there are the sparkling lights of Arona, a town that Liliana says is one of the best-kept secrets in Italy and hopes it stays that way. An antique clock on the mantel chimes eight o'clock. There's a knock at the door. Liliana, who's now dressed in her finest eveningwear for dinner, opens the door.

"Are you ready, my dear?" asks Signore Liliano.

"Yes." She turns toward Malarkey. "Are you ready, Malcolm?"

Malarkey is in the bathroom dressed in his usual attire,

but with a white T.J. Maxx dress shirt instead of his usual fading blue one, a slightly worn Oleg Cassini tie that he bought at Goodwill back in the 90s and the pinstripe sport coat he purchased at the thrift store. Otherwise, it's the same attire he always wears.

"Absolutely."

He arranges his tie and touches up his unkempt hair, slapping on some styling gel that will keep it from flying in distant directions. Liliana turns to her father with a half-smile and a shrug as if silently apologizing for Malarkey's appearance before the three of them walk down the stairs, led by Signore Liliano who holds Liliana's hand. They pass through the foyer and into the study, which is as opulent as the rest of the house with built-in mahogany bookshelves, stuffed with leather-bound books; a Steinway grand piano; Persian carpets on magnificent Macassar Ebony hardwood floors; and all the other accoutrements that go along with that kind of wealth. Malarkey doesn't really need to describe it all. The Reader should try to imagine what else is in the house since, quite frankly, it's the Reader's job to read and Malarkey's job to write.

As they walk in, there, sitting in a regal, high-back chair, dressed as if she were going to a ball, is Signora Liliano who looks exactly like her portrait. Liliana walks to her mother who deigns to stand. In the finest rendition of the *Real Housewives of Orange County*, they hug and air kiss missing each other's cheeks by millimeters. Malarkey follows respectfully behind.

"Mother, this is Malcolm."

He holds out his hand. She reluctantly holds out hers and they shake. The expression on her face is clearly one of disapproval and she makes no attempt to hide it. If the Reader has a good imagination, then the Reader can see the scowl on Jane Fonda's face since Fonda is the Queen of Scowls, *Barbarella* notwithstanding. So, just imagine Jane Fonda elegantly dressed, scowling at Malarkey and hold that thought.

"A pleasure to meet you," Malarkey replies, doing his best impression of Hugh Grant or maybe Jeremy Irons.

"Likewise," she answers as dryly as dryly can be.

She sits down, crosses her suntan legs and rests her arms on the manchettes, her hands slightly gripping the armrest as if she can hardly restrain herself. Much less anxious, Signore Liliano sits to her right as Liliana and Malarkey sit on a couch across from them. At that moment, a servant brings in a tray of sherry served, of course, in appropriate sherry glasses and offers them to everyone. Malarkey takes his and sniffs.

"Pedro Domecq. Amontillado."

"Pardon me?" Signora asks.

"The sherry. Reminds me of high table."

"High table?"

"At Oxford. Sometimes the dons would deign to invite lowly undergrads for a sherry before dinner."

"You attended Oxford?" she asks somewhat surprised.

"Yes. Christ Church College. Home of Lewis Carroll . . . the pederast."

Liliana discreetly elbows him. Malarkey turns to her as if he's done nothing wrong and shrugs his shoulders.

"What?"

"Liliana never mentioned that. How was it?"

"Stately, regal, regimented, and painfully pretentious."

Liliana gives him another slight "elbow."

"Ow!"

"And what did you study there?"

"Irish literature."

"And why did you choose that?"

He looks at Liliana.

"Because I liked to read and write."

Liliana smiles.

"I would like to make a toast," says Signore Liliano.

They all raise their glasses except for Signora Liliano who holds hers around chest high.

"To Liliana and Malcolm. May your trip be joyful and your time together bountiful."

The last part of that toast causes Signora Liliano to give Signore Liliano a scowl that clearly indicates her displeasure. Signore Liliano is used to his wife's scowling. After all, he's Italian and he's used to Italian women who are some of the best scowlers on the planet. He's actually said that to Liliana, but accords the comment to the late Lina Wertmuller whom he once met at an after party of the film, *Swept Away*. They all sip their sherry, except for Signora Liliano who grasps her glass tightly in her hands since she's more than a bit annoyed at her husband's toast. As a matter of fact, if she holds the glass any tighter it will shatter. More small talk ensues. Malarkey is not going to engage in that small talk, but the topics range from financial stuff to domestic stuff, career stuff to writing stuff. As Malarkey has written, "small talk" which can be defined as talk meant to fill the interstitial moments in our lives and which, depending on the length of said small talk, is time never again retrieved in one's life.

Subsequent to the small talk, they adjourn to the dining room, which is as opulent as everything else in the villa. Signore and Signora Liliano sit at opposite ends of a majestic mahogany table that looks as if it were used in *Downton Abbey* while Malarkey and Liliana sit across from each other. The table is heavily laden with china and crystal decanters of water and wine, but dinner is spent in relative silence except for the clinking of silverware against the plates or the splashing of wine being poured. Malarkey often looks at Liliana and Liliana often looks at Malarkey and Signore and Signora often look at each other, but very little is spoken and what is spoken is very pedestrian: the weather, Aneilli pasta, Arona, Bucatini pasta, the lake, Campanelle pasta, Ditalini pasta and every other alphabetical kind of pasta until Ziti. More small talk.

Of course, Malarkey can liven up the conversation by talking about how he and Liliana got caught fucking in a lavatory by the Chancellor of his university, not once but twice, but that's a bit more pedestrian than Malarkey thinks appropriate. Clearly, it's more pedestrian than Liliana thinks is appropriate. The Reader can only imagine how Signore and Signora Liliano would react to the news that their daughter was caught fornicating in a KLM lavatory even if it were business class. So it goes.

After dinner, the women and men pair off and go their separate ways. Liliana and her mother return to the study, Malcolm and her father head for the patio. Liliana sits across from her mother. Between them is a small table with a decanter of water. To say one could cut the tension with a knife would be a cliché so Malarkey will not say one could cut the tension with a knife. Signora Liliano stares at Liliana's engagement ring.

"I noticed your ring at dinner," Signora Liliano says with only a half-scowl.

"Yes. It belonged to his mother."

"Why did you not tell us?"

"I wanted it to be a surprise."

"That it was. Then this is not a joke."

"Why would it be a joke? I love him."

"Do you now?"

The Reader can clearly hear Jane Fonda deliver this line. Brilliant.

"Yes, I do."

"What do you love about him?"

"I love his wit, his intellect and his honesty."

"But has he been truly honest with you?"

"About what?"

Signora Liliano merely shakes her head.

At the same time, Signore Liliano and Malarkey are sitting poolside. Between them is a decanter of Calvados. Malarkey offers Signore Liliano a cigar, which he brought from the US for just such an occasion as this.

"Care for a Cohiba?"

"Yes, grazie."

He lights Signore Liliano's cigar and then his own.

"These are Cuban. Once upon a time, if you got caught smoking them in the US it was a fine and a prison sentence. Can you imagine? For smoking a cigar?"

"Then you should enjoy them all the more. Calvados?"

"Thank you, I will."

Signore Liliano pours him a glass of *Coeur de Lion* 1959 Vintage Calvados and Malcolm sips.

"This is terrific Calvados."

"Glad you like it."

"May I ask you a personal question?"

"Of course," Malarkey answers with a puff.

"How old are you?"

"We're probably the same age." He puffs. "Mid-fifties."

Signore Liliano raises his eyebrows.

"Fifty-fifteen. Why do you ask?"

"You're obviously aware of the age difference between the two of you."

"Is there an age difference? Hadn't noticed. Some people don't see color. I don't see age differences."

"Can we talk seriously?"

Malarkey shifts gears, and the tenor of his voice changes with his expression.

"As long as it's a serious question. Don't want to waste time answering non-serious questions."

"What do you want from her?"

"Want from her? Whatever she's willing to give me."

"Meaning?"

Malarkey leans in.

"Meaning, at my age, I no longer expect anything. She entered my life as a knock on my door. Maybe she'll leave that way as well."

"I noticed the engagement ring."

"It belonged to my mother."

"Then you're serious about this?"

Malarkey puffs and looks Signore Liliano straight in the eyes.

"It belonged to my mother," he answers, emphasizing the word "it" about as seriously as one can answer a question and pausing in between each word. Malarkey raises his eyebrows. Signore Liliano gets it.

"May I ask you another personal question?"

"As long as it's personal. Nothing worse than answering impersonal questions."

"How's your health?"

"Why do you ask?"

"Because we're old."

"And?"

"And my guess is we may suffer from the same malady."

"Would that be ED or old age?" Malarkey asks, puffing.

"It would be cancer."

The Reader can only imagine where the conversation goes after that. It isn't as if they are going to exchange prostate prognoses to see which one has a better chance of outliving the other or what degree of cancer each one has or what they fear most: having the prostate surgically removed or getting a semi-annual rectal exam. What the conversation does do is bring two men, who share a common and often lethal disease, together. Nothing unifies the seemingly un-unifiable than two of the Four Horsemen of Apocalypse, disease and death, being discussed by two men who are quite aware of two of the Four Horsemen of Apocalypse if not three of four. One can intellectualize that we are all made from the same carbon atoms of the cosmos, but until science discovers the answer to aging, we are all ineluctably tumbling headlong into the maw of mortality. With that thought in mind you might want to pour yourself your own Calvados as we return to the mother and daughter reunion taking place in the study.

"Did you set a date?" Signora Liliano asks.

"Not yet."

"And did you move in?"

"No, we've kept our homes for the time being."

There's an extended and uncomfortable silence, but the elephant in the room is getting anxious and no one wants an anxious elephant in one's room especially since elephant turds are enormous and quite difficult to clean up.

"What about children?"

Having spent as much time with Malarkey as she has, Liliana wants to answer, "As a concept or a recipe?" but she stifles herself.

"What about them?"

"Your clock . . "

"Is ticking. I know, mother."

"It is not a theory, Liliana. You have already had a miscarriage."

"I'm well aware of that."

"But . . ."

"But what?"

"He is old."

Liliana is used to hearing such things, from friends, from other students, and she's used to the looks they get when she and Malarkey are out in public with people staring at them and coming to the *obvious* conclusion that she's "fucking him for the money." However, Malarkey has no money so there's obviously something else at work that even Malarkey doesn't fully understand. Liliana used to get angry about it, indignant that others might be passing judgement on her, but then she decided to "fuck it" as Malarkey suggested. Regardless, at this point she doesn't really want to hear it.

"So are you," she answers with a bit of that disdainful residue and returns a scowl that can only be called "genetic."

"But I am neither a widow nor childless."

"What's that got to do with it?"

"I have raised my family and so has he. You have not. Do you think this will last?"

"I'm not a fortune teller, mother. I never thought Massimo would die in an auto accident and neither did you. I never thought I would have a miscarriage and neither did you. I never thought I would meet Malcolm and, I'm certain, neither did you."

"All the more reason to be concerned."

"I think I know what I'm doing."

"I just want you to be happy. Are you happy?"

"Yes. Are you?"

"I am. I just wish I could be happier for you," says Signora Liliano as she sips a glass of water.

After the discussions end and after the goodnights have been gratuitously spoken, Malarkey and Liliana go to bed.

"So, was your evening as unforgettable as mine?" Malarkey asks.

"She's not easy to deal with."

"No, really. I would never have thought that. Then I had the better evening."

"Why?"

"Because your father and I have a lot in common."

"Really. Like what?"

"The three 'c's. Cohibas, Calvados and . . . cancer."

Liliana ponders that comment.

"He shared that with you?"

"Yes."

"Then you should feel privileged."

"Because?"

"Because he'd share that with very few people. Maybe it was the Calvados."

"And not me?"

"You go without saying."

He turns to her and they kiss. Liliana is too tired to make love and, for that matter, so is Malarkey. It's a tiring journey and the dinner is not a respite from that. So, as is their normal bedtime position, Liliana turns on her left side and Malarkey spoons her with his right hand cupped around her breast. It isn't sexual for Malarkey nor is it sexual for Liliana. Perhaps, for Malarkey, a cupped breast brings him closer to the world of maternity. After all, Malarkey is an orphan. For Liliana, a cupped breast gives her a kind of solace and warmth in a villa that for all its regal opulence is somehow bereft of both.

CHAPTER THIRTY-EIGHT

THE BENTLEY;
OR SEX WITHOUT BORDERS

Early the next morning, the Reader finds Liliana and Malarkey drinking Lavazza and eating croissants at a kitchen table as the kitchen staff scurries around the scullery preparing food for later. Malarkey isn't going to describe the kitchen. The Reader should imagine what Mario Batali's kitchen might look like. If the Reader cannot imagine what Mario Batali's kitchen might look like then the Reader should Google Mario Batali's kitchen. Mario enters and immediately walks up to Malarkey.

"Signore Malcolm, I have talked with Signore Liliano and he agreed to let you drive the car whenever you wish."

Malarkey can hardly restrain himself.

"Grazie mille, Mario."

Mario leaves.

"Did you hear that?"

"What I heard was impossible," Liliana answers in between sips of Lavazza.

"What do you mean?"

"No one drives that car but Mario. It must have been the Calvados."

"Or my charm."

"As I said, the Calvados."

Malarkey rushes through whatever breakfast there is to rush through, grabs Liliana before she's had time to chew a croissant let alone swallow it, and after he gets some driving tips from Mario climbs into the driver's seat. It's a crisp, sunny, late-December morning in Arona. The sky is clear. From there, one can see Monte Rosa in the distance in all its magic mountain majesty. From Malarkey's point of view, the snow-capped peak appears to be smiling. For Malarkey, it's the conjunction of space and time and a moment that does not come that often. Malarkey gazes at Liliana and raises his eyebrows. Driving a Bentley: something he had not imagined on a "bucket list." And not just any Bentley, but a Flying Spur. Who could ask for more?

After a final driving tip from Mario, Malarkey adjusts the seat, the mirror, whatever other accoutrements need to be adjusted before he starts the car. The engine merely hums. Then he turns on the radio. As they slowly drive off the estate, one hears the finale of Rossini's "William Tell Overture." [Once again, to get the true flavor of this chapter, reading it to Rossini would be mandatory. Malarkey suggests the Reader listen to (https://www.youtube.com/watch?v=c7O91GDWGPU)].

At this point, the Reader should imagine aerial shots of Malarkey driving off the estate before engaging the winding eleven miles or eighteen kilometers (depending on whether you're an American or not) from Arona to Stresa along the shore of Lago Maggiore. Malarkey isn't going to describe the journey from Arona to Stresa along the shore of Lago

Maggiore since there are no words that can accommodate the beauty of the lake and the sky and the Alps, but as Malarkey drives, he broadly smiles at Liliana. She's not quite sure about Malarkey's driving skills since he looks more at her than at the road, which, at some moments, becomes a bit disconcerting. Each turn he makes parallels Rossini's music not unlike his driving exuberance in the car he drove in Carmel. The Reader follows his turning and winding, dipping and rising from Arona to Stresa along the shore of Lago Maggiore until Malarkey enters Stresa proper where he gingerly avoids hitting oblivious pedestrians and irresponsible Vespa drivers while navigating through phone-flashing tourists until they arrive curbside at the Regina Palace Hotel.

Now Malarkey could attempt to describe the Regina Palace Hotel in the manner of Thomas Mann, but as he's said he's not Thomas Mann and even if he were Thomas Mann a Thomas Mann description would take up a lot of pages and since the Reader is probably more interested in what happens at and after the Regina Palace Hotel, Malarkey believes an image would suffice. So, here's a shot of the Regina Palace Hotel:

After Malarkey pulls up to the front of the hotel, Rossini ends. It's incumbent upon the Reader to time the ending of the Rossini piece to coincide with the exact arrival time of Malarkey and Liliana at the Regina Palace Hotel. If not, please start over. But at the precise moment Malarkey parks, he holds up his hands from the steering wheel as if it were on fire and looks at Liliana.

"Fuck!!!!!"

Liliana merely raises her eyebrows, but doesn't react. After all, it's only a Bentley. Malarkey and Liliana decide to have drinks at the Regina Palace bar that overlooks the lake and from there they can see Isola Bella only four hundred meters away. If the Reader isn't familiar with Isola Bella, then, oh never mind. Malarkey nurses a Guinness Bitters; Liliana, a dirty martini made with Belvedere vodka and blue-cheese olives. It's a wee bit early for alcoholic beverages, but one needs to seize the moment in Stresa since those Stresa moments may not ever come again.

"Mario was right?"

"About what?"

"Driving the car."

"What about it?"

"It is better than sex."

"Excuse me?"

"He said driving it was better than sex."

"Maybe for you," Liliana says as she sips her martini.

Now this might appear to be a rather benign comment, but, for Malarkey, the wordsmith, no comment is really benign unless it's a comment without words and only punctuation marks, in which case that's already been done by a Brazilian writer. The Reader may detect a not so subtle irony on Liliana's part. One might assume that it's a dig at Malarkey's sexual performance or lack of one. If one assumes that's the case, then one is probably correct.

"Uh, what's that mean?"

"Not sure you want to get into it, do you?"

"Is there a problem?"

"There's often been kind of a problem."

"With what?"

"Malcolm, it's a glorious day in Stresa with the shimmering blue lake and the snow-capped Alps and peacock flocks on Isola Bella. Let's keep it that way."

Of course, Malarkey can't keep it that way even with it being a glorious day in Stresa with the shimmering blue lake and the snow-capped Alps and peacock flocks on Isola Bella and so he needs to taint the glorious day in Stresa with the shimmering blue lake and the snow-capped Alps and peacock flocks on Isola Bella by stating,

"Wait a second. You said it's *often* been a problem?" Malarkey asks, slightly agitated.

"Yes. On and off."

"Then why haven't you said something before?"

"Because before it wasn't the most important issue."

"And now it is?"

"To some degree."

"What degree?"

"You know."

"No, enlighten me."

"You don't have the . . . endurance."

"Are you talking about having sex or running a marathon?" he quizzically asks.

"I knew this would happen."

"What would happen?"

"You'd just get defensive talking about it."

"Who's getting defensive?" Malarkey defensively asks.
She rolls her eyes.

"It is a bit personal, isn't it? I mean I've tried almost
every med known to the sildenafil world."

"Then maybe you should try a different med or . . ."

"Or what?"

"Or try something else."

Malarkey's eyes get wide.

"Like what? A dick injection?"

Liliana raises her eyebrows, smiles, sips her martini,
but says nothing. Malarkey does not see that coming.
For Malarkey, the rest of the day is somewhat tainted and
Malarkey and Liliana don't talk too much. Even the lun-
cheon at the Ristorante Pizzeria Mamma Mia doesn't lift
the mood. It's not a secret to Malarkey that things aren't
as good as they could be and the slow decline in his performance hasn't gone unnoticed. The inability to perform
sexually goes beyond the physiological. Intercourse is, after
all, a psychological function as well. The two work hand in
hand, so to speak.

As dusk falls on Stresa, they return to the Villa. Malarkey
drives the winding eleven miles or eighteen kilometers from
Stresa to Arona, but unlike the earlier trip, when he turns
on the radio the Reader hears an instrumental version of the
"Song of the Volga Boatman." [To get the full flavor of what
Malarkey was feeling on the way back, Google (https://
www.youtube.com/watch?v=YZ6QJWpkvzs)]. Obviously,
the "wind is out of the sails" on the return trip and as the
Reader might imagine that parallels the music. What a twist.

After kilometers of silence, Liliana finally says:

"I've arranged for Mario to drive us to Milan tomorrow," Liliana says.

"Fine."

"Something wrong?"

"No, nothing. Never felt better."

"I thought you wanted to spend New Year's Eve in Milan."

"I did."

"And?"

"And now I'm not sure."

"Why not?"

"Performance anxiety."

"Are you serious?"

"Nevermore."

Liliana says nothing more for the rest of the drive, but the remainder of the page is left blank in case the Reader would like to write what Liliana might be thinking.

CHAPTER THIRTY-NINE

AT THE GRAND HOTEL ET DE MILAN AND AFTER

This is the famous Boldini painting of Verdi that regally rests in the foyer of the Grand Hotel et de Milan. One cannot visit Milan without being affected by Verdi and it is no different in Malarkey's case, as the Reader will discover anon. The hotel attendants take their luggage up to Verdi's Suite where, later that evening, Malarkey dresses up to look like Verdi with the same scarf and top hat, which he purchased in the Verdi Gift Shop downstairs.

"Lil, do I look like Verdi?"

Liliana finishes dressing and looks at Malarkey who's posing as if he were Verdi.

"Yes, but without the talent."

The comment stings Malarkey.

"Right. Grazie."

Liliana catches the *faux pas*.

"You know what I mean. Musical talent."

"Right. Musical talent. Of course. What else could it be?"

Though Malarkey has a penchant for Mahler, when it comes to opera, no one surpasses Verdi and Malarkey has read some of the best books on Verdi: Phillips-Matz biography; Osborne's *Complete Operas*; Willis's *Verdi's Shakespeare* and on and on and on. In some ways, Malarkey admires Verdi more than any other composer for a myriad of reasons some of which will become clear in a subsequent chapter. However, before they leave for dinner, Malarkey returns to wearing his usual garb since he doesn't want anyone to confuse him with Verdi.

It's a relatively chilly New Year's Eve in Milan. Clear skies. 4 degrees Celsius or 39 degrees Fahrenheit depending on whether you're American or not. Arm in arm, Malarkey and Liliana walk the few blocks to the Ristorante Rigolo for dinner a very unpretentious restaurant as the photo would indicate:

It's not exactly a hole in the wall, but one might mistake it for one; however the food is magnificent. For appetizers they share Oyster Britain, tuna tartarina with chives and raw shrimp; for first dishes, Liliana orders Risotto alla Milanese expressed with marrow and saffron while Malarkey orders Gragnano spaghetti with seafood and zucchini; followed by Redfish for two with potatoes and olives all accompanied by Brunello di Montalcino 2007 Tenute Silvio Nardi; and topped off with pineapple carpaccio with berry cream for Malarkey and a lemon sorbet with vodka for Liliana. Malarkey is hungry just thinking about what Malarkey ate. After dinner, they nurse a couple of Verduzzo Toblar of Venice Giulia 2008, but even though the dinner was superb, there seems to be a palpable tension in the air. Malarkey could say one could cut the tension with a knife, but that would be redundant so he won't.

"What's wrong?" Liliana asks.

"Can't put my finger on it."

"Can you put it on me?"

"I could, but it might be pointless."

Malarkey smiles sheepishly.

"Talk to me, Malcolm."

"Words escape me at the moment."

"We've not made love since we've been here."

"I'm aware of that. I apologize."

"I don't want an apology. I want you."

There's a "pregnant pause" during which time Liliana makes a face that reflects something isn't quite right, but not necessarily with the lack of lovemaking or entrées.

"Damn!" Liliana quietly shouts.

"Damn what? I said I'm sorry."

"No, I have to take care of something. I'll be right back."

She gets up and rushes to the toilet where she wipes herself only discover blood on the toilet paper.

"Fuck."

Still sitting on the toilet, she starts rummaging through her purse for a tampon or a reasonable facsimile, but can't find one. She looks again at the blood on the toilet paper and pauses. It is, after all, a reminder of her miscarriage and the fact she's still not pregnant as she closes in on thirty-seven. It's not a "bucket list" kind of look, but it is a look of waning expectations. If not waning expectations, then losing expectations. It's the look of a woman who understands that diamonds may be forever, but eggs are not. She anxiously returns to the table.

"Let's go!"

"Why? Haven't finished my Verduzzo Toblar."

"Fuck the Verduzzo Toblar, we have to go!"

"Right."

Malarkey hastily pays and they scurry out of the restaurant and walk briskly down Largo Treves. Liliana is in a rush. Malarkey tries to keep up.

"Lili, what is it?"

"My period."

"So?"

"So, I have no tampons. Is there blood on my skirt?"

Malarkey takes a look. There's no blood visible, but he admires the view.

"No, but your ass looks . . ."

"Not the time, Malcolm, not the time."

Liliana rushes into a nearby pharmacy near the Duomo as Malarkey waits outside looking toward the plaza while workers finish setting up the fireworks for that night outside the Duomo. Momentarily, Liliana walks out.

"Better?"

"It's not like a cold, Malcolm."

They walk back to the hotel in relative silence. Malarkey doesn't have to tell the Reader what Liliana is thinking since the Reader should know what Liliana is thinking. It was alluded to in the toilet. If the Reader has forgotten, please return to the toilet scene and re-read the paragraph. As for what Malarkey is thinking, it's debatable. No doubt he's thinking about what he's going to write in the chapter dealing with what Liliana is thinking. Regardless, the tenor of the time isn't very festive and any plan they have for celebrating New Year's Eve at or near the Duomo is as lost as the night itself. From their hotel window, they can see the fireworks exploding from the Piazza del Duomo and hear the residue of live concerts. But Malarkey stands in a bathrobe, hands locked behind his waist, looking at the festivities. Liliana lies on the bed. It's one of those silence is deafening moments that Malarkey will probably not write about—at least not in this novel. Maybe the next. Or the one after. As a matter of fact, New Year's Eve comes and goes.

After all, New Year's Eve really isn't much of an eve and as Malarkey's father once told him, "What everyone is celebrating is that they've survived for another year with or without Guy Lombardo." Regardless, he walks over to her and they kiss, but it's more celebratory than amorous.

"Do you love me?" Liliana asks.

"Yes, I love you."

"Then why don't I feel like you love me?"

"What would that look like?"

"You're so good with words, Malcolm, why not with feelings?"

"Because words are easy to write and easier to erase."

"And feelings?"

"Feelings have a short shelf life."

"So do some relationships."

Malarkey turns and looks over his shoulder.

"I am what I am, Lili. I don't know any other way to be."

Malarkey climbs into bed and she snuggles next to him.

"Malcolm?"

"Yes".

"I'm sorry I said those things about, you know, about Verdi."

"No apologies where none are necessary. I'm certain that Verdi wasn't offended."

She puts her head on his shoulder and closes her eyes. There's no need to go into the details of what they're feeling at that moment since Malarkey has alluded to it. Liliana slowly seeps into that slumber that belies something comforting as Malarkey continues to watch the fireworks and as they slowly dissipate into a kind of confetti of multi-colored detritus, he too falls asleep.

And then, Malarkey has a dream, a dream that haunts

him to this day. It takes place in the dining hall of Christ
Church College, Oxford. There's a banner that hangs from
the ceiling that merely reads "𝕽eunion," but of what type
it's not stated nor is there a year. It's a black banner with
white letters, written in large Old English font with the letters R and n smeared as if the letters had little time to dry.
He remembers that very clearly. The hall is filled with men
and women of Malarkey's age, all of them wearing black,
but not just black, but a faded black, a black dyed in the
colors of mourning and all of them have aged much more
than Malarkey, have aged to such a degree one might say
they're on the verge of looking macabre.

His peers appear to be in positions of frozen time, frozen
in poses of walking, of eating, of talking, of everything but
laughing or smiling or enjoying what one might consider the
reason for attending a reunion. Even the once most attractive of them, the women for which he may have been the
most enamored, have now surrendered to the fatigue of age.
Malarkey, dressed as he usually is, that is, somewhat shabbily, carelessly, with a faded-green corduroy sport coat with
patched elbows, a fading blue work shirt, missing buttons,
faded jeans, makes his way between and around his peers
being exceedingly careful not to bump into them for fear
they will fall and crack or splinter or dissolve into the atoms
that they are. A cold wind makes a shrill noise howling in
and out of the paneled dining hall as Malarkey walks with
trepidation toward the opposite end of the dining room. The
long tables have been removed and what is in their place
are round tables with black linens and black-draped fold-
ing chairs, black utensils, glasses filled with black liquid. It
reminds Malarkey of a novel by Huysmans.

At the end of the room, where the high tables would be, Malarkey sees Liliana standing in the middle of the riser, but she's not the Liliana he knows and loves, instead, she's a Liliana who looks remarkably like Miss Havisham: dressed in rich materials, satins, lace, and silks, but all in an aging yellow-white. She wears a long yellow-white veil, her white hair adorned with dried bridal flowers. Some bright jewels sparkle on her neck and on her hands while other jewels lay on a table beside her. She only wears one shoe, the other is missing; her hose is snared and holey; her veil is but half arranged and shreds of lace cover her breasts. Trinkets lay on the table next to her engagement ring exposed through parchment. Malarkey approaches her, but as he does, she stands expressionless. Her expressionlessness doesn't deter him. In his excitement to see her, he rushes to and embraces her. She embraces him as well, but when he pulls her closer to him, she suddenly decays and, like sand in an hourglass, sifts in fragments to the floor, a floor in which she only exists as a pile of yellow-white detritus.

Startled awake by the nightmare, Malarkey looks longingly at Liliana as a way of reconstituting her being, of making her whole again, climbs out of bed and sits in a chair by the window. Malarkey gazes at Liliana who's sleeping peacefully unaware of the almost palpable horror Malarkey has just experienced. Malarkey puts his hand over his mouth and continues to look at her until he passes out and sleeps fitfully until dawn. After he awakes, he dresses as Liliana continues to sleep. He kisses her on the forehead and leaves the hotel room.

CHAPTER FORTY

AN UNSCHEDULED MEETING
AT THE CASA VERDI

It's rainy, chilly. Gloomy enough for Milan in January. The
Reader might ask, Where might Malarkey be going on
such a day? On New Year's Day? To that, the Reader will
soon discover. His journey is not serendipitous. There's a
reason for his walk, alone. Malarkey wraps a scarf around
his neck, doffs a navy blue newsboy cap and leaves the hotel
nodding as he does to the portrait of Verdi. One can hear
the sound of workers cleaning the New Year's Eve debris in
the piazza. On his walk, he finds a vendor selling flowers,
buys a small bouquet of roses and continues to walk with
purpose toward the Casa Verdi, Verdi's final resting place.

When he approaches the Casa Verdi, there is something
severe yet sumptuous, imperfect but orderly and symbolic,
and upon entering, Malarkey wishes he could sing opera as a
way of praying, just as Verdi did. Verdi rests here along with
his wife, Giuseppina Strepponi, beside him. The maestro's
descendants have supposedly said that he had thought about
situating his tomb at his beloved villa at Sant'Agata, and

that after having chosen the Rest Home as his final resting place he had explained to his relatives: "I'm eliminating the bother of having too many people coming to visit me at your home after I'm dead!"

At that time of day, on that type of day, Malarkey walks through a Casa Verdi bereft of visitors, of tourists, of other aficionados until he comes upon the maestro's crypt whereupon Malarkey kneels, places the bouquet next to the crypt, then stands with clasped hands in front of him at the same instant Verdi appears dressed as he is in the Boldini painting.

"Thank you for the flowers. It is very kind of you to bring them on such a gloomy day," Verdi says.

"Thank you for the music."

"I do not think you came just to thank me for my music and leave a bouquet of flowers, no?"

"No."

"Then why else are you here?"

"I wanted to ask you why you had no more children after yours had died."

Even in death, Verdi has to compose himself. Perhaps, Malarkey should ask something else, but Malarkey is often as oblivious as he is delusional.

"My wife and my children were my only solace as a failed composer."

"But you weren't a failed composer?"

"At the beginning, yes, a very failed composer. A most failed of failed composers."

"But there were extenuating circumstances, maestro."

At that moment, Verdi becomes very nostalgic, one might say emotional. To call the deaths of his wife and children "extenuating circumstances" was a polite way for Malarkey not to force Verdi to regurgitate the tragedies of the past unless it is Verdi who wishes to do so. It's common knowledge, that while he was composing *Un giorno di regno* both his children fell ill and died. His daughter, Virginia, was born on March 26, 1837, and died in August, 1838; his son, Icilio, was born on July, 11 1838, and died on October 22, 1839. Both children, babes in arms, had already died before *Oberto* was produced. Soon after those deaths, his wife, Margherita, contracted encephalitis and died as well. And while he grieved, he also had to write.

Contrary to what Malarkey thinks, Verdi is very open about how those deaths affected him and his work. It's as if Verdi wants to compensate Malarkey for his visit on that cold and gloomy January day and so Verdi recounts how he recovers from those multiple tragedies and the events leading up to the composition and performance of Nabucco.

"*Un giorna di repo* failed to please me. Certainly, my music was partly to blame, but partly, too, the performance. My mind was tormented by the tragedies in my life and I was embittered by the failure of my work. I was convinced that I could find no consolation in my art and decided never to compose again."

"But you were only twenty-six?"

"It didn't matter. At that moment, nothing mattered to me. I had lost my wife and my children. Nothing seemed important. I eventually wrote to Merelli and asked for my release from the contract."

"Merelli?"

"Merelli was the manager of the La Scala. He sent for me and even in my grief treated me like a child. In retrospect, maybe I was. He would not allow me to be discouraged by the failure of my last opera, but I was adamant about quitting. Merelli shrugged his shoulders as if he could do no more and handed the contract back to me as he said: 'Listen, Verdi! I can't force you to write. My faith in you is undiminished. Who knows whether, one of these days, you won't decide to take up your pen again? In that case, as long as you give me two months' notice before the beginning of the season, I promise that your opera shall be performed.' I thanked him, but those words had absolutely no effect on my decision and I left. Artists respond to failure in many ways. Some fine renewed inspiration in their work; others, like me at the time, just wanted to quit. I am sure you know about what I mean, Signore Malcolm."

"How do you know my name?"

"The dead know everything about the living."

"Then you already know my future question to you?"

"In due time, Signore Malcolm. In due time. I took rooms in Milan at the Corsia dei Servi. I was still grief stricken and had essentially given up thinking about music let alone writing about it. How could one think about something as frivolous as music after losing my entire family? But one snowy, winter evening on leaving the Galleria De Cristoforis I accidentally ran into Merelli, who was on his way to the theatre. Taking me by the arm, he asked me to accompany him to La Scala. On the way, we talked about pedestrian things and he told me he was in difficulties over a new opera he had to present. Merelli had entrusted it to Otto Nicolai, the conductor and founder of the Vienna Philharmonic, but the latter was dissatisfied with the libretto by Solera."

"Imagine!" said Merelli. "A libretto by Solera! Magnificent! Epic dramatic situations and beautiful verses!

But that pig-headed composer won't hear of it and says it's a hopeless mess of a work. I'm at my wits' end to know where to find another one quickly."

"Of course, Merelli was a marvelous psychologist. I do not know whether he had rehearsed the possibility of meeting me at some point, but he knew exactly what he was doing when he shared that information with me and without thinking, I automatically replied:

"I will help you out myself."

"Yes, yes. Didn't you submit *Il proscritto* to me?"

"I have not written a note of the music, but it is yours if you want it."

"Oh! Marvelous, what a stroke of luck! Who would have imagined it?"

"When we reached La Scala, Merelli told the stage-manager, Bassi, to look immediately in the archives for a copy of *Il proscritto*, which, as you know, is based on the play *Hernani* by Victor Hugo. The copy was there. At the same time, Merelli picked up another manuscript and, showing it to me, exclaimed:

"Look what I found! It's Solera's libretto. Such a beautiful subject. It's hard to believe that imbecile Nicolai turned it down! Go on take it. Give it a read and tell me what you think."

"What in the hell should I do with it? No, no, I have no wish to read librettos. I am finished! I told you that! It would be a waste of my time and yours."

"Go on! It won't do you any harm. Read it and then bring it back after you've finished. It will give you something to read during these frigid Milan nights. You can't go to Pasticceria Marchesi every night."

He handed me the manuscript, which was written on large sheets in big letters, as was then customary. I rolled them up, said goodbye and returned to Corsia dei Servi. On the way, I felt a kind of indefinable malaise, a profound sadness, a distress that filled my heart almost to the point of bursting. When I got to my room I threw the manuscript on the table with such anger that I thought I may have damaged them. But as I stood over the scattered pages I noticed one page in particular was staring up at me and I was drawn to the line: "Va, pensiero, sull'ali dorate."

"Fly, thought, on the golden wings."

"Correct, Signore Malcolm. I am impressed with your Italian."

"Pigeon Italian."

"Maybe, but Italian nonetheless."

Malarkey was still a bit overwhelmed by the fact Verdi knew his name, but then he remembered what Verdi said about the dead.

"I read through the verses that followed and was moved not only by the content, but the writing I thought to myself could Nikolai be that wrong about the work? As you may know, Solera was an accomplished writer whose style was very much influenced by Manzoni and with whom I collaborated a lot. I continued reading because the lines were almost a paraphrase from the Bible, and thought I am not that religious, the reading of Bible had at times delighted or lifted me. I read one passage, then another. Then, that antagonistic voice within me reminded me that I was done with writing and that the only antidote to failure was never to write again. If one never writes, one is never exposed, so I tossed the libretto aside and went to bed.

"But it was no use. You must know, Signore Malcolm, that once an idea infects your mind there is no remedy but completion. I couldn't get *Nabucco* out of my head. Unable to sleep, I got up and read the libretto, not once, not twice, but three times, so that by the morning I knew Solera's libretto by heart. Not a line, not a phrase, not a word did I not know. Regardless, I was not prepared to relax my unwillingness to write and that same day I returned to the theatre and handed the manuscript back to Merelli.

"Isn't it beautiful?" he said to me, smiling as if he knew I slept not a wink.

"Very beautiful!"

"Well then, if you think it is beautiful then set it to music!"

"No, absolutely not. I will not hear of it. I am done!"

"Go on. Set it to music! I know you are dying to do that! Are you not?"

"And so saying he stuffed the libretto into my overcoat, took me by the shoulders and not only pushed me out of the room, but locked the door in my face. What was I to do? Of course, it was all premeditated. From that snowy evening the night before, Merelli knew exactly what I would do and so I returned home with Nabucco in my pocket. How conniving.

"Of course, I could not contain myself. One day I wrote one verse, another day another I wrote another verse, here a note, there a phrase, little by little the opera was composed. It was the autumn of 1841, and recalling Merelli's promise, I went to see him and announced that *Nabucco* was finished and could therefore be performed in the next Carnival season. But there was a problem. Even though, Merelli was ready to keep his word, he also pointed out that it would be impossible to stage the opera in the coming season, because the repertory was already settled and because three new operas by renowned composers were due for performance. To arrange a fourth opera by a composer who was a novice was dangerous for everyone not the least of which was me. He said it would be better to wait for the spring season, for which he had no prior engagements and he assured me that good artists would be hired. But I refused. I was angry. He had promised me and I had done the work so I demanded that he either stage during the Carnival season or not at all. There were good reasons for saying that, since I knew it would be impossible to find two other artists as excellent as la Strepponi and Ronconi, whom I knew would be engaged and on whom I was much relying.

"Merelli, although disposed to agree with me was, as impresario, not altogether mistaken. To stage four new operas in a single season was very risky not to mention adding another by a bonafide failure. But I had stood firm. In short, after assertions and denials, obstacles and half-promises, the bills of La Scala were posted, but to my shock, *Nabucco* was not announced! I was outraged.

"Even at twenty-six and grieving over the loss of my family, I was hot-blooded. I wrote a rude letter to Merelli, venting all my resentment. Of course, in a way, I was lashing out at him because of my own failures, my own insecurities, not only as a writer but also as a father and a husband and was blaming him for my own tragedies. I must confess to you, Signore Malcolm, that as soon as I had sent the letter I felt remorse, and I feared that as a result of that hastily written missive I had ruined everything: our friendship, my connections to the opera world, my future as a composer. But Merelli was insightful and he sent for me, and when I arrived at La Scala he exclaimed:

"Is this how you write to a friend?"

I started to apologize when he interrupted me.

"But still, you may be right. We'll stage *Nabucco*. You must remember, however, that I have enormous expenses because of the other new operas. I shall not have the resources to build special scenery or sew original costumes for *Nabucco*, but shall have to patch it up with whatever we can find best in the storerooms. Agreed?"

I agreed to everything because I was anxious for the opera to be staged. New bills were issued, on which I finally read, *Nabucco*! Toward the end of February the rehearsals began, and twelve days after the first rehearsal the first public performance took place, on March 9, with Strepponi and Bellinzaghi and Signori Ronconi, Miraglia and Derivis in the cast."

"And it was a success."

"Yes, it was a success as was Solera's *I Lombardi alla prima crociata*, which followed."

"So, you owed it all to Merelli."

"Yes, he understood me well."

Verdi pauses.

"I realize that I have been doing all the talking. I apologize, Signore Malcolm. Is there something else you want to ask of me?"

"Yes."

"And what would that be?

"I have been writing for years and regardless of what I've been told, I feel as if I'm a failure."

"And why is that?"

"Because I'm old and gray and full of sleep and haven't achieved what I set out to achieve when I was young and vibrant and infected with the joy of composition. Those who know me don't know the anguish I suffer and of being relegated to some repository of worthless prose. Sucking on the tit of obscurity."

Verdi paused.

"Yes, well I must commend you on your colorful use of metaphor, Signore Malarkey, and I do not mean to speak in clichés, but an artist must yield to his own inspiration. I should compose with utter confidence a subject that set my musical blood going, even though it were condemned by all other artists as anti-musical. In short, an artist cannot endure on the vagaries of others."

"But I'm an old man."

"But you are not a dead man."

"Then what advice can you give me?"

The maestro thought for a moment.

"I have given you my advice, Signore Malcolm. My story is my advice. Take from it what you wish."

"But you had Merelli as your mentor."

"Yes, and now you can consider me, yours. And if anyone asks, you can tell them, I get my advice from Giuseppe Verdi. I hear la Strepponi calling so I must leave you, but I thank you for the flowers, my friend, and I wish you well."

Malarkey respectfully nods to the maestro and turns to leave.

"On second thought I do have a few words of advice."

Malarkey looks back.

"Yes? And what is that?"

"See Falstaff."

And with that, Verdi disappears into the vastness of the universe filled with the atoms of all the other musical miscreants who in spite of allegations and assaults their melodies haunt us still.

CHAPTER FORTY-ONE

WHAT MALARKEY GLEANED FROM WATCHING FALSTAFF

Life is a burst of laughter, so, be happy hereafter.
Your mind is a tempest whirling, always this way and
that.
Everyone mocks you, whether you're thin, or whether
you're fat.
But it is best for him who has the last laugh of all!

This loses something in translation. Malarkey suggests the Reader see Verdi's opera in either English or Italian for the full impact of what Verdi suggested. Only then might one appreciate the maestro's words.

CHAPTER ETERNAL

AT THE TOMB OF THE UNKNOWN HUSBAND

Before Malarkey and Liliana return to Citrus City, Liliana makes a visit to the gravesite of her husband, Massimo. She goes alone, with a bouquet of white lilies, kneels at the graveside located beneath an isolated medlar tree whose drooping branches, contorted by the winter winds, shrouds the tombstone which reads:

𝔐𝔞𝔰𝔰𝔦𝔪𝔬 𝔙𝔢𝔯𝔤𝔞

1971 -2009

𝔅𝔢𝔩𝔬𝔳𝔢𝔡 𝔥𝔲𝔰𝔟𝔞𝔫𝔡, 𝔇𝔲𝔱𝔦𝔣𝔲𝔩 𝔖𝔬𝔫

Liliana recites a prayer, heard only by Liliana, kisses the marble headstone and leaves the cemetery to the accompaniment of the wind whistling through the meager, yet melancholy, medlar leaves.

CHAPTER FORTY-TWO

ENTR'ACTE; OR, GAZING OUT A WINDOW AT THIRTY-FIVE THOUSAND FEET

This is another *entr'acte* because it comes in between leaving the shores of Lago Maggiore and returning to the senescence, if not the detritus, that is Citrus City. It is also reflective of what will be a change in Malarkey's worldview as the following dialogue between Liliana and Malarkey will attest:

"Gotta see the dentist about this tooth," Malarkey says.

"Which tooth?" Liliana answers.

"Wisdom."

"To put one in or take one out?"

Liliana smiles and raises her eyebrows.

"You're still not a member of the mile high club. You wanna try it again?"

"On two conditions."

"What's that?"

"One, that you're absolutely positive the Chancellor is not flying on this plane and two, you get me pregnant."

There's a pregnant pause.

"Gotta see the dentist about this tooth."

"Always an answer," she replies as she gazes out the window at thirty-five thousand feet. Additional tests to follow. Watch for that chapter.

END PART II

ACT III

WHEN YOU ARE OLD AND GRAY AND FULL OF SLEEP

"If you do not love me I shall not be loved. If I do not love you I shall not love."

—Samuel Beckett

CHAPTER FORTY-THREE

COMING IN A CUP & OTHER IMAGINATIVE THINGS ONE CAN DO WITH SEMEN

At this point, the Reader may be drawing conclusions about Malarkey's character. Some may be angry with him; some may call him an asshole; some may think there's little hope for Malarkey and Liliana to remain as a couple let alone as parents; while some others may have already thrown the novel into the trash or flung it to the floor or hurled it out the window, even a closed window, or tossed it through the slats of the Venetian blinds or crumbled it into molecules and atoms. The Reader might think Malarkey has no interest in whatever Liliana wants, but Malarkey implores the Reader not to judge him harshly. Then again, Malarkey really doesn't give a fuck what the Reader expects; however, if that is what the Reader expects then the Reader would be wrong as the Reader can plainly see Malarkey walking down a hallway at Kaiser Permanente toward a sign that reads: UROLOGY LABORATORY TOILET. Malarkey is not walking into the Urology Laboratory Toilet because he has nothing better to do than hang out in the Urology

Laboratory Toilet of Kaiser Permanente. He's there for a reason.

With some trepidation, Malarkey walks into the toilet, locks the door (there's a first for everything) and raises the toilet seat. Malarkey isn't quite sure the Reader has any notion of how it feels to walk into a urology lab toilet, whip out one's dick, wipe it off with a sterile pad and begin to jack off with the hopeful expectation that something of significance will be ejaculated. Besides the fact the toilet is sterile and the pad is sterile and the containers are sterile, the entire act of coming in a cup leaves one questioning whether it's supposed to be an orgasmic experience or merely a clinical one. The context is everything. Needless to say, after a significant amount of prompting his dick to cooperate, not to mention an even more significant amount of time fantasizing (this would include, but not be limited to, Malarkey conjuring all sorts of erotic fantasies as a way of imploring his flaccid phallus to erect itself [e.g. images on PornHub, aging fantasies of a youthful Sonia Braga or Romy Schneider or Jean Seberg or Julie Christie *ad astra*]) Malarkey, as if by the miracle of hand, succeeds in coming into the cup, squeezing out every drop as if it were a Maxwell House commercial, hurriedly zips up, returns the sample to the laboratory and flees the clinic as if he's stolen the pharmacy's entire inventory of Oxycontin or feeling as if he were Peter Lorre with the letter "M" (for masturbator) indelibly sewn on the back of his jacket. What then remains are the test results. In a way, it's a bit like waiting for the SAT or GRE results while fidgeting as if on steroids.

Sometimes, being competent at one's job has reverse consequences. This is the case with the urology laboratory.

Malarkey is hopeful the results of his masturbatory miscreance are going to take some time. Maybe a week. Maybe longer. Maybe they will get lost. But, Malarkey is wrong. As a matter of fact, later the same night Malarkey sits at his laptop when he receives a message from the lab that reads:

YOU HAVE TEST RESULTS.

Malarkey hesitates since he's not quite sure he wants to know the results. Are his fellas Olympic swimmers or are they merely floating in a sea of semen like jetsom upon the ocean? Gathering courage, Malarkey finally clicks on the attachment which takes him to the test result site. He clicks again and in bold letters, the results appear on the screen, which reads in a discourse that is easy to understand:

Sample shows no sperm content, no motility, no morphology. Ability to conceive: negative. Possible lab error. If not, you have a lot of drowned swimmers. Please return for follow up analysis and have a nice day. ☺

Malarkey looks at those results with mixed feelings, since Malarkey didn't want to have the tests done in the first place. The Reader may not understand why that is, but, you see, there's a direct correlation between the content of one's sperm and, with all due respect to Dr. King, the content of one's character. Regardless of one's physical stature, one's health and well-being, one's sperm content is more reflective of one's manhood than one's ability to bench press one's weight and the results of Malarkey's sperm count is: zero. It is the closest thing to menopause a man can come to (no pun intended) and Malarkey ponders what, exactly, the results mean. For Liliana, the results could be devastating. After all, the Reader knows she's desperate to get pregnant and, at least at the time of the results, Malarkey cannot impregnate a termite assuming termite impregnation were even possible. This impotence affects Malarkey on multiple levels not the least of which is the realization that whatever fantasy he envisioned about starting another family at his stage of life it is merely that: fantasy.

Additional tests to follow. Watch for that chapter. With that in mind, Malarkey turns his attention to something into which he can sink his teeth.

CHAPTER FORTY-FOUR

IN THE DENNTAL OFFICE OF DR. AL-KHWARZIMI, PERSIAN ORAL SURGEON

Malarkey isn't kidding about the tooth. He has been avoiding the extraction since his twenties, but removing a wisdom tooth at his age is not a simple thing. There can be extreme medical consequences: nerve damage, infection, dry sockets, even death. Look what happened to Wilt Chamberlain a week after he had a wisdom tooth removed: dead. So, Malarkey arrives at his appointment with some trepidation and the Reader sees him agitatedly sitting in the dental chair in the office of Dr. Al-Khwarzimi, oral surgeon, when Al-Khwarzimi, a mid-fifties, dark-skinned, Persian, walks in. It's a state-of-the-dental-arts kind of operatory. Tastefully decorated in a kind of high-tech way, but with a distinctly Persian motif running throughout the office: Persian carpets, a facsimile of a portrait of Fath Ali Shah Qajar and original paintings by Hossein Behzad and Jazeh Tabatabai among others.

"Good morning, Malcolm."

"Doctor."

They shake hands and as Dr. Al-Khwarizmi talks, he washes his hands while his assistant prepares hypodermics and other supplies needed for the surgery.

"How's teaching?"

"Couldn't be better. Another year has come and gone and they haven't fired me."

"And your writing?"

"Couldn't be better. Another year has come and gone and I haven't murdered any New York publishers."

"And your daughter?"

"Couldn't be smarter and unlike Donald Trump I have absolutely no interest in having sex with her."

Al-Khwarizmi raises his eyebrows.

"So, are we finally ready to have that ancient wisdom tooth removed?"

"Didn't know I had a choice?"

"You don't, really, but I always give my patients the right of first denial."

"That's a good line. Could I steal it?"

"Hadiyati Lak."

"Sorry, my Farsi is a bit weak."

"My gift to you."

"Sepaas."

"You're welcome."

Al-Khwarizmi sits in his dental chair, adjusts the dental light and after Malarkey opens his mouth the doctor uses his dental explorer to poke around in Malarkey's mouth as if looking for a reason to operate when, in fact, there isn't one. Usually in those moments, dentists like to ask questions a patient cannot answer with a mouthful of dental equipment. And the questions are not merely questions that require a simple "yes" or "no," no, they're more like: "So, what cost-effective opportunities to achieve significant reductions in carbon pollution, including promoting more energy efficient homes and businesses, improved industrial practices, and cleaner sources of energy might you propose?" or "What suggestions might you make in relation to Kierkegaard's inversion of Feuerbach's critique of Christianity?" or "Given the late Diego Maradona's obesity, especially in the film *Youth*, what dietary suggestions would you have offered him?" Those sorts of questions. So, in order to circumvent that possibility, Malarkey initiates a conversation before the doctor can ask.

"Did you know there was an Al-Khwarizmi who invented algebra?"

Al-Khwarizmi looks at him askance as if someone had asked Malarkey: "Did you know Bushmills was Irish?" Like it's bloody obvious.

"Yes, it's something we all learn as children," Al-Khwarizmi's replies.

"Fascinating."

"Only to Westerners. Malcolm, I'm going to give you an injection of midazolam."

"What's that? Sounds like a Walter Scott novel."

"It's an anesthetic that will make you drowsy so you shouldn't feel a thing."

"Sounds like a Walter Scott novel. Is there a way I could get that every day? You know, around 4:30?"

"No, Malcolm. I'm afraid not."

The doctor's assistant prepares the injection; Al-Khwarizmi injects it into Malarkey's arm and hands the syringe back to his assistant.

"Just relax for a while, Malcolm. I'll be back in a few minutes."

Al-Khwarizmi leaves and Malarkey slowly closes his eyes. In his anesthetic haze, Malarkey has a dream. In the dream, Malarkey is wearing the same blue work shirt he always wears, but it's beneath a black suit fashioned after one worn by Baudelaire before he lost his inheritance. Just where that vision comes from, Malarkey can't tell the Reader though, perhaps, it's from his idolization of Baudelaire when, as an undergraduate, Malarkey slept with a copy of *Les Fleurs du Mal* beneath his pillow or how he would memorize lines from Baudelaire's poetry to try out on potential girlfriends or how he would visit Baudelaire's grave in the Cimetière Montparnasse and leave real bouquets before removing the plastic ones and dumping them in the trash. Who knows? The Reader would have to ask Malarkey. Regardless, in the dream, Malarkey stands behind a podium the front of which bears a plaque that reads: PULITZER PRIZE. Malarkey addresses the audience.

"When I was young, my father, who never graduated from high school, taught me to take risks. The greater the risk, he used to say, the greater the reward. But one had to be cognizant of failure as well since failure always precedes and coexists with success, but at that point when failure has no emotional effect on one's identity, on one's reason for being, on one's self-worth, then, and only then, could one consider himself a success. I always remembered that advice and one of the greatest risks one can take is to become a writer since the successes are few and the failures are legion.

"But it's not merely the rejection. Rejections are bits of paper or indifferent emails, boilerplate emails, emails conceivably sent from people whose knowledge of letters may be tantamount to a dolphin's knowledge of the chemical composition of water. No, it isn't the rejection per se, but the psychological effect of the rejection which, after decades and decades of rejections, one tends to question one's being, questions whether the decades spent in exhuming those words that impede one's daily existence is worth the trauma of awaking. Perhaps, that's why I weep at hearing Beethoven's ninth knowing he heard no response, no adulation, for the notes that consumed him. It becomes the same for a writer who languishes in a kind of misery of oblivion knowing that whatever one writes may end up in the compost of critical neglect. Perhaps, Gogol and Kafka were right. Self-immolation through the incineration of one's life's work. What a lovely way to burn.

"I recall a quote from Verdi, who amid the grieving of the deaths of his children and wife, amid the grieving over his failures as a writer, said: 'I adore art . . . when I am alone with my notes, my heart pounds and the tears stream from my eyes, and my emotion and my joys are too much to bear.' It is the legacy of all artists to suffer for their work. Whether in the garden of oblivion or in the weeds of success.

"Let me end by saying I would like to thank the Pulitzer Committee for this most prestigious of awards. It is a very humbling experience and let me thank the committee for recognizing that though writers of my ilk may be long in the tooth, we are not necessarily short on talent. Thank you."

In the background, the Reader might hear people applauding, but that's really the end of the dream. The sound one really hears is not that of applause, but of the aspirator sucking saliva from Malarkey's mouth. Malarkey slowly awakes from the "twilight zone" he's been in and as he opens his eyes, Dr. Al-Khwarizmi appears in a kind of purple haze.

"Things went very smoothly, Malcolm. Here's a prescription for Vicodin in case you need it. If there are no complications I'll see you in a week."

"Thank you," Malcolm slurs, feeling that one side of his face is drooping significantly lower than the other side of his face and the oral surgery has left him completely transfigured which, in fact, could improve his chance of getting published. A kind of, "Je suis Quasimodo."

Al-Khwarizmi starts to leave, but stops at the door and turns.

"Oh, and by the way congratulations," he says.

"For what? Malarkey asks as he squints."

"For the Pulitzer. Well deserved."

Al-Khwarizmi walks out and Malarkey looks rather sheepishly at his assistant.

"Did I . . . ? Malarkey asks the assistant.

"Yes, you did."

"Should I apologize?"

"Not at all. Happens all the time," the assistant answers. "Why just last week a patient was here who under anesthesia mumbled that he had walked in on Little Red Riding Hood fornicating with the Big Bad Wolf in his bathroom. Crazy, huh?"

Malcolm smiles sheepishly.

"Yeah, crazy."

CHAPTER FORTY-FIVE

JUST WHEN YOU LEAST EXPECT IT . . .

The next morning Liliana and Malarkey sit at her breakfast table, Malarkey's right cheek is still slightly puffy from the trauma of the day before, even though the Vicodin produces a certain amount of forgetfulness depending on what one exactly wants to forget. But today it's not about Malarkey. It's a doubly special day: Valentine's Day and Liliana's birthday. Malarkey believes she did that intentionally in order to receive two gifts instead of one, but Liliana convinces him he should stop reading tweets by Sarah Palin and Michele Bachmann about the lame stream liberal conspiracy regarding the origins of holidays. So, she opens the Valentine's card.

"Hope you like it. It's unique," Malarkey says.

In some kind of floral design, the front of the card reads: "Say it with flowers." Liliana flips the card open and it reads in letters designed with flowers: "B(Eat) my Valentine! Love, Malcolm."

"Well?"

"How thoughtful. Did you buy this before or after taking the Vicodin?"

"Thought you'd like it. Even Hallmark couldn't come up with that."

"No, I imagine not."

"Go on, open it."

She unwraps a gift that only Malarkey could have wrapped since its crushed corners, salvaged Scotch tape and re-gifted holiday ribbon have Malarkey's name written all over it.

"I see you did your customary creative gift wrapping job."

"Yeah. Brilliant, no?"

Liliana removes the re-gifted ribbon and the crushed paper revealing a small cardboard box about 5"x7"x3" which she opens and gingerly removes the tissue paper exposing about a dozen edible thongs. She takes them out one by one: red ones, yellow ones, orange ones, fuchsia ones, magenta ones, multicolored ones. It isn't what she expects.

"Well, wadya' think?" Malarkey asks, as if he's just handed her the Hope Diamond.

"I'm . . . I'm speechless."

"Thought so," Malarkey says proudly.

"Just have a question."

"What's that?"

"Isn't this the same gift you gave me for Christmas?"

"Well, yes, but I thought we ran out of them."

"We?"

"Okay, me, but these have different flavors. The lavender ones taste like blueberry. The beige ones taste like cheese-cake and the pink ones, wow, the pink ones taste like pussy."

"Pardon me?"

"Pussy, you know, pussy."

Liliana feels like asking: "Whose pussy?" but educated in decorum and refined taste, she refrains from doing so.

"I'm not even going to dignify that comment with a question, but how do you know what they taste like?"

"Well, I had a sample."

Liliana rubs her forehead.

"I'm not going to ask which one."

"So, what do you think?"

"I think I have to think about it."

"Okay, you think about it and let me know what you think about it. Gotta run to class."

"Bye."

She dangles the thongs in her hand and shakes her head as if she can't believe it, but before Malarkey leaves, he stops.

"Oh, how foolish of me. I almost forgot."

He walks back to her and takes out another Malarkian-wrapped, small box from his sport coat."

"Happy birthday. I love you." He kisses her. "Gotta run. See you at the Citrus."

Malarkey rushes out and she unwraps yet another Malarkian-wrapped package gift in which there's a small white box that reads: MONT BLANC. She opens it to discover a Meisterstück 149 Fountain Pen. Being Malarkey, Malarkey leaves the price tag on it: $1,000 which renders Liliana somewhat speechless. Given Malarkey's penchant for buying inappropriate gifts for appropriate occasions and vice versa, the Reader might think Malarkey doesn't know what he's doing. If so, then the Reader is as stupid as Wilson. Malarkey sincerely hopes that's not the case since there is absolutely no hope for Wilson.

CHAPTER FORTY-SIX

FS&G: FAMOUS NEW YORK PUBLISHERS

After his class, Malarkey brushes off the cobwebs on his computer, sits at his monitor and reads an email from a Mrs. Rasmussen:

Dear Professor Malarkey, it's urgent that you come to my office on the first to discuss your grossly delinquent Effort and Management Time form.

Sincerely, Mrs. Harriet Rasmussen
Assistant to the Vice President for Delinquent Faculty Forms
Citrus City College
Citrus City, California

Malarkey pauses for a moment since he has no fucking clue what an EMT form is. What he does know is the administration often comes up with those forms in order to make the lives of tenured faculty members discomfiting. Make that all faculty members. Malarkey often emails the Chancellor with queries as to why there's such an obsession with the administration in creating a fecundity of forms for faculty to fuck up, but the Chancellor generally ignores his emails or summons Malarkey to his office to explain to him that he runs a university and not a Malarkey fan club. Fair enough even though the latter comment always piques him to his core since he's never had a fan club. Regardless, Malarkey doesn't know who Mrs. Rasmussen is, but he does know who Mike Tyson is and Malarkey Googles him. Just why he Googles him will be revealed to the Reader in a subsequent chapter.

After returning home, and before meeting Liliana, Malarkey walks into his kitchen, grabs a bottle of Bushmills from a cabinet, sits down at the table and pours himself a shot as he sorts through his mail and discovers a letter that has his name and address on it with a return address of that most prestigious New York publishing house:

FORTZ, SHIKKER, AND GANIF

Malarkey looks at the Reader and raises his eyebrows, then takes another shot of Bushmills.

"Right."

He stares at the envelope and as he does, he hears a cacophony of voices of both men and women layered over each other like the layers of a soundtrack and which dissolve into each other repeating the same phrase scalded into the hippocampus of memory:

"Dear Mister Malarkey, we are sorry to inform you . . ."

Dear Mister Malarkey, we are sorry to inform you . . ."

Dear Mister Malarkey, we are sorry to inform you . . ."

Dear Mister Malarkey, we are sorry to inform you . . ."

Dear Mister Malarkey, we are sorry to inform you . . ."

Dear Mister Malarkey, we are sorry to inform you . . ." *ad
mortem*. To say the very least, if Malarkey has received
one of these letters he's received thousands of them written
by frustrated English majors from Dartmouth or Brown or
wherever whose expectation of working for a New York
publisher and discovering that s/he is the next Harold Ober
has slowly decayed into what it truly is: a sixty-hour work
week for frustrated English majors from Dartmouth or
Brown or wherever whose expectation of working for a
New York publisher and discovering that s/he is the next
Harold Ober or Maxwell Perkins provided s/he know who
Ober and Perkins were.

And after virtually listening to thousands of these dis-
embodied voices (i.e. the real soundtrack of Malarkey's
life) they eventually merge into one, before Malarkey takes
another shot of Bushmills, rips open the envelope, removes
the letter and begins to read.

FORTZ, SHIKKER AND GANIF

Dear Mr. Malarkey, We are sorry to inform you that after
a reading of the chapters from the novel *The Mad Diary of
Malcolm Malarkey* we cannot offer you a contract to publish. Unfortunately we do not publish campus novels.

Regards, blah, blah, blah.
Acquisitions Editor, Fortz, Shikker and Ganif

Malarkey pours himself another shot, downs it, then puts
the glass down and walks out of the living room. Moments
later, the Reader hears Malarkey scream from the kitchen:

"FUCK!!!!!!!!!!!!!!"

That outpouring of emotions is followed by the sounds of crashing plates and broken glass accompanied by the Beatles' "I'm a Loser," if not in real time, than in fictional time, emanating from his record player. What also accompanies that outburst is the fact that Malarkey accidentally cuts his hand while picking up the broken glass that he threw to the floor in reaction to the excitement of getting yet another rejection. You get the picture.

So, before sharing the "exhilarating news" with Liliana, Malarkey goes to the hospital to have his hand attended to: several stitches to close a slice near the hypothenar muscles. Fortunately, it was his left hand, but while there, he does what he should have done long ago and far away and that is take another semen sample that he was supposed have taken when he was informed there might have been a mistake. Malarkey believes that because of the news he's received from Fortz that it might have a negative effect on his sperm sample. Malarkey thinks there's a connection between his rejection and, due to some kind of "trickle-down theory," it will change the outcome of the test. But as Malarkey has often said, Malarkey is often delusional.

At the same time, Liliana is on her computer sending Malarkey an email that reads: I'M LATE. Liliana has her finger on the mouse. Her finger is raised above the mouse. It hovers. She hesitates, but doesn't send it. Now one can debate what the phrase, "I'm late" actually means. It could mean she's "missed her period" or that "she anticipates being late for dinner." If the latter, Malarkey thinks it should read "I'll be late." If the former, there may be multiple reasons for that to happen including stress, but Malarkey will leave any deconstruction of the phrase "I'm late" to the Reader since Malarkey believes the Reader is perspicacious and doesn't need any prompting from him.

Later that evening at the Citrus, Malarkey shares his bad news with Liliana (who is on time and which lends credence to the former interpretation) and creates a ludicrous fictional reason why his hand is wrapped in gauze since the truth is so embarrassing.

"Cut it shaving"

"Shaving? How do you cut your hand shaving?"

"Oh, happens all the time. I was changing blades and I accidentally cut my hand."

"Really."

"But enough about me. How was your day?"

And they proceed to celebrate both his latest rejection and her birthday by ordering two filet mignons and a bottle of Romanee Conti, 1986. After sharing a Grand Marnier Soufflé, they return to Liliana's house where they begin with the foreplay of kissing, move on to cunnilingus and fellatio, and consummate it all with the old in-out-in-out and Liliana riding Malarkey like "Prairie Rose" Henderson on a bareback bronco. Of course, Malarkey, anticipating the possibility of such a ravenous rodeo, increases his sildenafil dosage verging on an overdose in hopes of being inflicted with the alleged side effect of a four-hour priapism. If one has to overdose what better way to do it.

CHAPTER FORTY-SEVEN

DEAR GIUSEPPE

February 15

Giuseppe Verdi
Casa di Riposo per Musicisti
Fondazione Giuseppe Verdi
Piazza Buonarroti 29
Milano, Italy

Dear Maestro, had to share my good news with you. As my mentor, you should know that I recently received word that my novel, *The Mad Diary of Malcolm Malarkey*, was rejected by Fortz, Shikker & Ganif in the United States. I shall continue to persevere and I owe much of that to your supportive words and encouragement. I shall forever be indebted to you for that.

Abbracci,

Malcolm Malarkey

CHAPTER FORTY-EIGHT

DEAR MALCOLM

February 24

Dr. Malcolm Malarkey
Dept. of English
Citrus City College
Citrus City, California

Dear Dr. Malarkey, Maestro Verdi is out of the country. We will share your news with him when he returns. In the meantime, in the words of a famous Italian-American, do not give up, do not ever give up.

Regards,

Giuseppina Strepponi
Assistant to Signore Verdi

CHAPTER FORTY-NINE

WHERE HAVE YOU GONE, MIKE TYSON, MALARKEY TURNS HIS LONELY EYES TO YOU, KOO-KOO-KA-CHOO

B ut there was little time for self-pity since Malarkey was summoned to appear at the Office of Faculty Effort and Time Management to talk to Mrs. Rasmussen, a pudgy, mid-fifties woman with a too-tight chignon, Trotsky-like glasses, and matronly dress one might see on *The Waltons* and who, as she glances over some documents on her desk, tries not to stare at Malarkey, who is sitting patiently waiting for her to react to the Mike Tyson inspired tattoo perfectly plastered on the left side of his face. Clearly, Mrs. Rasmussen is unnerved by Malarkey's appearance even though she tries not to stare at Malarkey's homage to Iron Mike, whose philosophical wisdom Malarkey often quotes in class, his favorite being: "Everybody's got plans until they get hit." Genius.

"Should we get down to business then?" Malarkey asks, rubbing his hands together and pretending to shadow box.

"Yes, now, Professor Malarkey it's . . . it's come to our

attention that your, your annual faculty effort and time management form is overdue."

"What is that? I have no clue."

"It's a form that indicates how much effort you've put
into your teaching and research and how you've managed
your time."

"Yes, I gathered that from the title which reads Faculty
Effort and Time Management form, but what is it exactly?"

"I think I've stated that fairly clearly."

"Perhaps, but I've been at Citrus City College for almost
three decades and I've never filled out one of these."

"That's because it's a new form."

"Right, but if it's a new form then how is it overdue?"

"Well, it's not that new."

"Then how new is it?"

"Relatively new."

"That's a relative term. Just how relatively new is it? And
to what is that relative if not relevant?"

Malarkey rests his elbow on his thigh and blinks at Mrs.
Rasmussen with a smile.

"Maybe a year."

"I see, but what I fail to see is how I'm supposed to
account for my time and effort. How does one quantify
that?"

"Well, that's listed on the form. I can show you."

She opens her desk drawer and pulls out a form which
she nervously hands to Malarkey trying desperately not to
gawk at the Tyson tattoo. Malarkey scans it.

"So, as I read this, all my time has to be accounted for
including, say, trips to the toilet?" Malarkey asks.

"That, that's correct. There's a special column for the

number of times you go to the rest room and the amount of time you spend doing each."

"Each what?"

"You know."

"No, I don't. Could you clarify that?"

Mrs. Rasmussen clears her throat.

"Number one and number two," she whispers.

"Number one and number two!" Malarkey repeats loudly enough for the entire office to hear. "Hope everyone is clear about that!" "Of course. Number one and number two! How could I have mistaken those two numbers!"

"Yes," she replies *sotto voce* somewhat embarrassed by his outburst.

"Right. So, how, exactly, am I supposed to measure the time taken for my number one and number two?"

"I'm glad you asked."

She opens another drawer, takes out a plastic bag and removes a plastic stopwatch.

"You can use this."

She hands him the stopwatch.

"A stopwatch."

"Yes, all you have to do is account for the actual time you spend . . ."

"Doing number one and/or number two . . . ," Malarkey interrupts.

"Yes, and then log it in the appropriate column."

"Is there a maximum amount of time allotted for this or are we on the honor system? And do you want me to return the stopwatch? That's a bit sketchy."

Mrs. Rasmussen nervously adjusts her blouse.

"I detect a bit of sarcasm on your part, Professor

Malarkey. This, this is very important data collecting."

"Caca collecting?"

"Data collecting."

"No, not a drop of sarcasm on my part. Actually, I'll get started on this right away," Malarkey answers with feigned enthusiasm.

He grabs the form, stuffs the stopwatch in his corduroy jacket and starts to leave.

"Oh, one last question."

"Yes?"

"There doesn't seem to be a column for diarrhea. Should I add one or just bring in a sample?"

Mrs. Rasmussen doesn't answer and Malarkey skips out of the office.

If the Reader has been reading closely, then the Reader knows exactly what is to follow. As usual, Malarkey sits across from Chancellor Jones.

"Joe, it's April Fool's day. It's a fake tattoo."

Malarkey starts to rub it off though it doesn't come off easily.

"Fucking henna."

"Malcolm."

Malarkey is licking his fingers trying to get the tattoo off.

"Malcolm, it's March first not April first."

Malarkey looks at Jones somewhat confused.

"March first?"

"Yes, March first."

"Who would have guessed? Leave it to Stephen Hawking to fuck up time."

"Regardless, Malcolm, not everyone gets your sense of humor or your satire or your sarcasm."

"I wasn't being snarky. You know, the world would be a better place if it did. Even Jesus must've had a sense of humor."

"And why is that?"

"He had a yahoody mother, right?"

Jones folds his hands on his desk.

"Can I ask you a personal question, Malcolm?"

"Sure. As long as it's personal. I hate impersonal questions."

"Are you under some personal stress?"

"Personal stress. Personal stress. Hmmm. Let me think. Why do you ask that, my droog? Sounds hound-and-horny to me."

"That's what they say."

"That's hearsay, Joe. Even Judge Judy wouldn't accept that."

"But is it true?"

"Maybe. Some. A little. We're all under some kind of stress, aren't we? Who goes throughout a day without some kind of stress? At this point, having a bowel movement would cause me stress. What if takes too long and I go over the defecation time limit! Or put the time in the wrong column! Can you imagine the pushback from Mrs. Rasmussen?"

The Chancellor leans across his desk.

"Malcolm, I mentioned this to you last term, but I think you need to take that sabbatical. You earned it so you should take it."

"Is that what *they* think?"

Jones looks at Malcolm sympathetically.

"No, Malcolm, it's what *I* think."

Malarkey nods, but reluctantly.

"Will you think about it, Malcolm? Just think about it."

The following page is left blank for the Reader to think about what Malarkey may have thought about after meeting with the Chancellor.

THIS PAGE INTENTIONALLY LEFT BLANK EVEN THOUGH IT'S NOT

CHAPTER FIFTY

BETWEEN MARCH AND MAY; OR, ENTR'ACTE, PART III

Presumably, the Reader will want to know what happens subsequent to the Tyson fiasco and the end of classes. Except for the Karl Marx costume Malarkey wears to class on March 14 for which he is arrested and except for the leprechaun outfit he wears on St. Patrick's Day while he paints the Chancellor's office door green and except for the Muslim costume he wears to class on April Fool's Day for which he is arrested and except for the bloodied Vietnam Vet costume he wears to class on April 30 for which he is arrested and except for the Pancho Villa costume he wears to class on May 1 for which he is arrested, nothing of major consequence occurs between March and May; however, the relationship between Malarkey and Liliana is a wee bit rocky. But what relationship isn't? Is there a need to go into details? Let's just say there are some disagreements about Malarkey's future with Liliana and *vice versa*. The Reader already knows the details, but to recap, the Reader has to remember these are two people who are quite independent and so that independent nature is going to be tested if, in fact, they decide to get married, which, at this point, isn't happening. If the Reader has been in one of those relationships, then the Reader can imagine what transpires over those two months: she prefers the toilet seat down, he prefers it up; she doesn't like air conditioning, he can't live without it; she likes to sleep on her right side, he likes to sleep on his left; she says tomato, he says tomahto; she prefers the missionary position because of direct contact with her clitoris; he'll take whatever position he can get. You get the picture.

It's what happens when people of opposite genders who are wired differently spend a lot of time together. Liliana spends a lot of time on her studies occasionally asking Malarkey for some suggestions about books and such. Malarkey is eager to help and be supportive, but, over time, many of the books Malarkey suggests have gone out of favor, are considered passé even though the authors of said books were giants in their field. Leavis and Levin, Wellek and Warren, Auerbach and Lovejoy. It's irrelevant if those names mean anything to the Reader because they don't mean much to anyone else anymore either. So it goes.

Anyway, at some point, Malarkey does something very un-Malarkey like; namely, he visits Paolo not only to imbibe, but to chat about the love of his life: Liliana, not Bushmills. It's near closing time at Flann O'Brien's and Malarkey is talking with Paolo while sitting at the bar staring at the caricatures of Beckett and Joyce and Yeats all of whom seem to be staring back at him. Even though he's had one Guinness too many, Malarkey realizes that the caricatures of Beckett and Joyce and Yeats are actually listening to what he's saying and sometimes they offer advice which interrupts their dialogue.

"So, what's up?" Paolo says.

"I'm a wee bit stuck."

"What's the problem? Not my cousin?"

"No, your cousin is the best thing to happen to me in a long time. I'm not sure what I'd do without her."

"Have you told her that?" Beckett asks.

"Not in so many words."

"How many words?" Yeats asks.

"I'm much better at writing words than I am at speaking them."

"But this isn't a book, Malcolm," says Joyce.

"Point well taken, Jimmy."

"Jimmy?" asks Paolo.

"Jimmy. Jimmy said it wasn't a book."

"Oh, right, Jimmy said that."

At this point, it should be clear that what Malcolm sees and hears is not exactly what Paolo sees and hears.

"Maybe you should try it."

"Try what?"

"Speaking words."

"Communicating," says Beckett.

"That's a laugh coming from you, hah," says Malarkey.

"Tell her how you feel," says Yeats.

"Yeah, well, I can't write like you do, Billy B. Actually, I'm not sure I'm much of a writer at all."

"Why do you say that?" asks Paolo. "Weren't you getting that book published?"

"Changed their minds. It's gone."

"What's gone?" asks Paolo.

"Whatever talent I once had. Maybe there's nothing left to say."

"No pen, no ink, no table, no time, no quiet, no inclination," says Joyce.

"Happened to me," Beckett says. "You know with the eyes going and going and then going and going beyond and beyond the going to the ending, the ending of the beginning, going until and I can't go on, I go on and in the end, the end of it, it's gone."

"All empty souls tend toward extreme opinions," says Yeats.

"Yes, well, thanks fellas that cheers me up no end. I'll have another Black Nail."

"There is no such thing as a great talent without great will power," says Paolo.

"Yeah, but Balzac was a great plagiarizer."

"Then you have a precedent."

"I can't go on. I'll go on."

"Got it, Sam."

"You don't sound like the Malcolm I know," says Paolo.

"Maybe it's just a darker side of the Malcolm you know. Like being under a volcano."

"Let me go to hell, that's all I ask, and go on cursing them there, and them look down and hear me, that might take some of the shine off their bliss."

"Chill out, Sam!" says Malarkey.

"Maybe it's the alcohol talking," says Paolo.

"Maybe it's all the chuntering going on with Sam and Jim and Billy B. Guys never shut the fuck up. Gotta go," says Malarkey.

"Are you okay?

"Yeah."

"Ciao, Malcolm."

"Ciao."

Malarkey hops off the stool and tipsily starts for the door.

"Malarkey?" Beckett asks.

Malarkey turns.

"You're on earth. There's no cure for that."

Malarkey nods, walks out of the bar and silently staggers home through a shortcut of crooked crosses and headstones, on the spears of the little gate, on the barren thorns. His soul swoons slowly as he feels the rain falling faintly through the universe and faintly falling, like the descent of their last end, upon all the living and the dead. Malarkey thanks Jimmy J. and to the God of Public Domain for that bit of stolen prose.

Fortunately, Malarkey is able to secure the house key and open the door before the possibility of repeating his Basil Fawlty impersonation. Soon, he profoundly passes out atop crumpled copies of the *TLS* and the *New York Review of Books* that adorn his couch. What Malarkey is oblivious to is that those same periodicals will, in time, have reviews of his novel, which he will not want to read.

CHAPTER FIFTY-ONE

HELL HATH NO FURY
LIKE A WOMAN IGNORED

L ater the next night, the Reader finds Malarkey in his bathroom staring at the age spots on his hands. In the background, the Reader hears Mahler's *Symphony No. 5. IV Adagietto*, which, as the Reader remembers, Malarkey invariably plays when there's some agitation going on in his life, which seems to happen on a weekly, if not a daily, basis. The fact it's the same piece played in Visconti's *Death in Venice* is purely coincidental and Malarkey has no intention of contracting and succumbing to cholera whether it's in Venice or Citrus City; however, he does think about tuberculosis and how romantic a nineteenth century disease it was and how he would choose tuberculosis over any other debilitating disease if given the choice. Especially since it goes well with his black, Baudelaire suit. But back to the bathroom.

Malarkey turns his attention from his hands to his face and scrutinizes it: turning one cheek, then another, running his hand through his cropped white hair, looking at his neck, checking the age spots wondering how to get rid of them.

"God damn you're an old fuck, Malarkey. You're on earth, there's no cure for that, is there?"

There's a knock on the door.

"Gotta pee, hurry up."

Malarkey walks out and Liliana rushes in and drops her pants.

Malarkey returns to the living room and sits at his typewriter with his back to the Reader. After a few moments he stands up and walks off. The Reader lingers on a page in the typewriter which reveals the sentence: "Every word is like an unnecessary stain on silence and nothingness."

At the same time, Liliana sits on the toilet peeing. She looks again at the medicine cabinet now with a bottle of Vicodin in front of the plastic container meant for the semen analysis that was due several months earlier because of the fuck up in the urology lab. Liliana slowly leans over and opens the cabinet doors. She pushes away the Vicodin bottle that's in front of the plastic container and merely stares at it. Then, overtaken by what its emptiness means, begins to weep silently. The Reader should realize by now that the empty container is not the same container that Malarkey used to collect his semen initially, but a new container for him to come into. Also, Liliana does not know the secret between Malarkey and the Reader; namely, that Malarkey made a second trip to the urology lab for an additional test on the same day he had his hand stitched. Just why Malarkey doesn't tell her is a mystery even to Malarkey, but, as has been stated repeatedly, Malarkey is often delusional.

In his living room, Malarkey sits in a chair, legs propped on an ottoman, when he hears Liliana slam the bathroom door; rushes into the living room and hurls the container meant for his semen sample at him. He ducks as it whizzes by.

"What is that!"

"I'm hoping whatever it is it's plastic."

"Don't give me that shit! Why have you done nothing with it!"

"No time."

"No time! It's been in that cabinet for months. You told me you were going to do it months ago. Why didn't you do it!"

"Shit happens?"

"How could you do that to me! We talked about this! I trusted you to do it!"

"I know, but I went . . ."

"No buts, Malarkey! Don't I mean anything to you! Don't you love me enough! I would have done anything for you, Malcolm! Anything! I have done everything for you. I asked for a simple gesture on your part! Something that would show me you love me. But you failed even that."

"You do mean everything to me."

"So, why not this? You know how much it means to me. Why not this!"

"Because I fear being a new father is gone for me."

"Great. Now you tell me. After months and months. Do I have to admit that my mother was right! God forbid!"

"No, I've told you before. In so many words."

"You're so good with words on a page, Malcolm, but not from your heart! You're a dick, Malcolm. Testa di cazzo!"

"Perhaps. But it's hard to see myself as a hero by leaving a young widow and a fatherless child on this godforsaken planet."

"Now he waxes existential! I trusted you to do that for me!"

"Expectations . . ."

"Stop with the fucking quotes, Malcolm! You hide everything beneath that intellectual veneer!"

"It's the only veneer I have."

"God damn you, Malcolm!"

She picks up the plastic bottle and throws it at him again.

"It's just like you!"

"I don't disagree."

Liliana rushes him and starts hitting him in the shoulder. Malarkey does nothing.

"Brutto figlio di puttana bastardo!"

Crying, she puts her arms around him the way she did in his dream. He embraces her though it seems to be too little too late as he half expects her to disintegrate into a pile of wetted ashes. Distraught, she lets him go.

"I can't stay here. I can't. I have to leave. It's too much for me."

She grabs her purse and heads for the door.

"Goodbye, Malcolm."

"I love you," Malarkey says as she slams the door. There is no response to his words of affection as Malarkey stares at the plastic container now resting ruefully in a corner of the room. Her last words resonate throughout the house. Hell hath no fury like a woman ignored.

CHAPTER FIFTY-TWO

WHEN FACING THE TRUTH FAILS, TAKE A SABBATICAL

Two weeks pass and Malarkey has not heard from Liliana. It's springtime. The Reader knows this because the jacarandas are blooming, turning the streets of Malarkey's neighborhood into carpets of lavender and the college into a tent city in preparation for commencement. Malarkey always finds commencement a time of reflection since he often recognizes students he's had as freshmen graduating as seniors. It's a bittersweet moment for him since he senses the passage of time not only by the erection of tents and scaffolds, but by the fact students of students he has taught over the years are also the children of children he has taught over the years. A bit like Proust's madeleine with the difference being one should not eat students.

Regardless, there's a piece of parchment tacked on Malarkey's office door and scribbled in a font that tends to bleed on the page reads,

PROFESSOR MALARKEY WILL BE ON SABBATICAL FROM JUNE-FEBRUARY

There's a knock on Malarkey's door and Malarkey, a wee bit hung over from finishing yet another bottle of Bushmills the night before, catatonically sits at his desk staring at a computer screen the screensaver of which shows a picture of ships sinking in the Grand Canal of Venice, before he gets up and opens the door. To his surprise, it's Matthew.

"Professor Malarkey."

"Yes, yes, Matthew come in," he says, trying to shake off the residue of his hangover.

Matthew walks in.

"How are you?"

"Fine, thank you."

"Have a seat. What can I do for you?"

Matthew sits.

"It's the end of the year and I just came by to say . . . thank you."

"For what, pray tell."

"For being one of the best teachers I've ever had."

Malarkey is a bit taken aback by Matthew's comment since few students ever tell him that either in person or in writing. To the contrary, they usually write things on his evaluations such as, "Fire him immediately!" or "He thinks he knows more than we do!" or "He makes us read too much!" or "Why does he care about typos!" or, most cutting of all, "He's a lousy dresser!" The Reader gets the idea. So, for Matthew to say something like that to his face is tantamount to the Chancellor condoning Malarkey's behavior.

"It's very kind of you say that, Matthew. Thank you."

"No, it's been a privilege to learn from you and, and, I just wanted to tell you that in person."

"Well, you've done an excellent job with your work and I wish you a restful summer. You've earned it. What will you do after graduation?"

"I've been accepted to medical school thanks in part to your recommendation. I'd like to work for Doctors Without Borders eventually."

"Well, I commend you on that. It's an arduous journey, but you're more than capable of completing it and I'm certain you'll make an outstanding physician."

"I see you're going on sabbatical."

"Yes, I need a respite."

"From teaching?"

"From life."

"Where will you go?"

"I'm thinking about Trieste."

"Why there?"

"I need to go somewhere out of this world and the name of the city matches my mood at this time."

Matthew nods, puts his can of Red Bull on a nearby end table, fiddles around in his backpack and removes a small box.

"I wanted to give this to you."

Matthew holds out a pen box that boldly reads "Mont Blanc." Malarkey is surprised by the gift. He rarely if ever receives compliments about his teaching and even more rarely receives gifts. After all, the only gift an asshole should get is another asshole to replace the one he is.

"This is very thoughtful, Matthew. Thank you, but you shouldn't have . . ."

"Well, I have to get going, professor. See you at commencement."

Matthew gets up, quickly hugs Malarkey, grabs his backpack and starts to walk out.

"Goodbye, Matthew."

"Goodbye, professor."

Matthew closes the door and as Malarkey stares at the pen box, he becomes a bit emotional about it. As Malarkey ponders that moment, there's another knock at the door and Malarkey assumes it's Matthew returning for the can of Red Bull. He picks up the can and opens the door with a smile. But it's not Elmo; it's Liliana. They say nothing. Nothing needs to be said. She's been crying. Newly spawned tears linger on her cheeks. She merely hands him the engagement ring, wrapped in the same parchment in which she received it, kisses him on the lips, turns and leaves.

Malarkey stands in silence. His face registers a combination of disbelief and disappointment, results of a denial past and an emptiness that can never be registered in prose. Maybe poetry, but Malarkey isn't much of a poet so he's not going to wax poetic. Let's just say that awakened at four in the morning to the sounds of staggered footsteps outside, sleep avoids him. Perplexed, Malarkey allows himself to wander aimlessly in thoughts. Thoughts tangent to other thoughts, lost love, lost marriage, both of which arraigned in the court of love's mismanagement. It appears that Malarkey is destined for days of lost desire, isolated moments along the Schiavoni. Not Aschenbach on the Lido, but another autumn in Venice with a death of a different odor. He returns to his computer and stares at the sinking ships in the Grand Canal wishing he were on one.

CHAPTER FIFTY-THREE

THE PENALTY FOR LATE LAB RESULTS

"Sample shows no problem with sperm. Ability to conceive: positive. Swimmers not like Michael Phelps, but they won't drown either. Have a nice day. ☺"

CHAPTER FIFTY-FOUR

IF YOU DO NOT LOVE ME I SHALL NOT BE LOVED. IF I DO NOT LOVE YOU I SHALL NOT LOVE

Some weeks follow, and even though the two of them only think of each other, they never meet. Their days are filled with anxiety. One day, Liliana will walk by Malarkey's bungalow, look quickly at his house, but doesn't stop. On another day, Malarkey will stand outside Liliana's bungalow staring at it in the rain as if waiting for a sign, an omen, anything that will move him to knock on her door, plead for forgiveness, beg for another chance. Thunder is heard in the distance, but no omen appears.

On some Saturday afternoon, Liliana will stand outside a baby store called Jacadi, and look longingly into the window before entering the store and purchasing a scalloped collar body suit for a girl and a cotton piqué body suit for a boy. On a Sunday afternoon, Malarkey will return for a bike ride and sort through old photos of a young Andrea before putting them back in a box and walking out of the garage. As the Reader knows, this isn't the first time he's done that. At some point, this novel needs to end, but one asks the question, How?

Aristotle has written in his "Poetics" the end of a work is linked to the beginning with inevitable certainty and in the end, we understand the meaning of the whole. With that in mind, the Reader can return to the beginning of this novel. Imagine that you see Malarkey from behind as he stares out to sea. The shot looks almost like a postcard with Malarkey standing as a lone figure on the deserted white sands as the sun slowly sets on the horizon. The only sound you can hear is that of the sea breaking onto the shore. Now imagine your eyes as a camera that slowly approaches Malarkey and begins to circle him 180 degrees until you see him from the front: his white hair cut closely to the scalp, his white eyebrows, a shaggy white beard; he's dressed somewhat shabbily, carelessly, a faded-green corduroy sport coat with patched elbows, a fading-blue work shirt, faded jeans. He's pondering whatever needs to be pondered. Now imagine a moment later when Liliana walks next to him carrying their infant son in her arms. She holds the baby in her right arm, puts her other arm in Malarkey's, and kisses him as they both stare out to sea and as they do Malarkey recites Yeats to the Reader:

> Dance there upon the shore;
> What need have you to care
> For wind or water's roar?
> And tumble out your hair
> That the salt drops have wet;
> Being young you have not known
> The fool's triumph, nor yet

Love lost as soon as won,
Nor the best labourer dead
And all the sheaves to bind.
What need have you to dread
The monstrous crying of wind?

Malarkey imagines that the Reader isn't satisfied with this ending since it's Malarkey imagining. But beginnings and endings are the hardest things to write so, being incapable of writing an ending that might satisfy all Readers, Malarkey relies on one of his mentors and merely closes with this:

No symbols where none intended.

THE END

COPYRIGHT MARK AXELROD 2022

WATCH FOR VOLUME II

THE FALL & RISE OF MALCOLM MALARKEY

FOLLOWED BY VOLUME III

MALARKEY'S WAY; OR , LIFE AND DEATH IN THE TIME OF COVID

WORKS CONSULTED

Verdi's Falstaff in Letter & Contemporary Reviews, Edited and translated by Hans Busch, Indiana University Press, Bloomington & Indianapolis, 1997.

Verdi, The Man and His Music, Carlo Gatti, Translated by Elizabeth Abbott, G.P. Putnam's Sons, New York, 1955.

Verdi, A Biography, Mary Jane Phillips-Matz, Oxford University Press, Oxford, 1993.